Muncherjee Cawasjee

Prince Albert

Selections From the Prize Translation of a Gujarati Poem

Muncherjee Cawasjee

Prince Albert
Selections From the Prize Translation of a Gujarati Poem

ISBN/EAN: 9783337168117

Printed in Europe, USA, Canada, Australia, Japan

Cover: Foto ©Andreas Hilbeck / pixelio.de

More available books at **www.hansebooks.com**

PRINCE ALBERT.

Selections from the Prize Translation

OF A

GUJARATI POEM

Written in the year 1863

BY A PARSEE POET NAMED

MUNCHERJEE CAWASJEE. S. L., ALIAS "MUNSOOKH."

AUTHOR OF

GUNZ-NAMEH,—HAYVALAI ZEND AVASTA,—JUMSHIDE NOWROOJ,—PRINCE
ALBERT,—BAIT RITTEE,—DISCUSSION ON THE PARSEE LAWS,—SIR
JUMSHIDJEE BARONET,—TRANSLATION OF COUNT GOBINEAU'S
METHOD OF READING CUNEIFORM TEXTS,—MOONTAKHEBA
SHAH NAMEH,—SHARE AND SUTTABAJI,—AND
NAM-SATAYESHNE.

The Translation by W. H. HAMILTON,

TUTOR TO SONS OF SIR J. JEJEEBHOY, BART.

Published at the BOMBAY EDUCATION SOCIETY'S PRESS,
JANUARY 1870.

PRICE RS. TWO.

BOMBAY:

PRINTED AT THE EDUCATION SOCIETY'S PRESS, BYCULLA.

PREFACE.

THE TRANSLATION, from which the following Selections are taken, was finished in November 1864; and was that to which a prize, offered in April of that year, for the best translation of the whole of Munsookh's Gujarati Poem on Prince Albert, was awarded. The original poem is a very long one; and its translation is probably twice or thrice as long as the whole of these Selections. For a variety of reasons, which need not here be enumerated, the publication of the translation was delayed; and even now it has been thought better to publish, at first, these Selections only, rather than, at once, the whole Translation.

The original poem has been largely read by the Gujarati-speaking portion of the Native community of this Presidency; and it has been thought that the presentation in English dress, to English readers, of Native ideas regarding several European institutions, such as are treated of in the poem, will be neither uninteresting nor unprofitable.

With regard to the Translation, it may be remarked that the aim of the translator was, above all things, to give a *true* translation. He did not seek to alter anything, or make use of language any where which should convey a meaning differing by even a shade from what he conceived to be the meaning of the author. Of course he does not presume to think that he always succeeded in rendering the exact thoughts of the author into English : it was, however, his constant effort to do so.

The style of the Translation is, in most places, ordinary prose ; and in others a kind of rhythmical prose, supposed by the translator to be not altogether unlike the style of the Poetical Books in the English Bible, and of the well-known poems of Ossian. It is only Songs and Hymns, in the original poem, which have been rendered in this style.

Selections from the Translation, such as it is, are now for the first time submitted to the public.

W. H. HAMILTON.

Bombay, 1st January 1870.

SELECTIONS

FROM

THE TRANSLATION OF A POEM ON

PRINCE ALBERT.

The Name of God.

In the name of GOD, the Great and the Ancient, who is wiser than the wisest, who in his
essence is merciful. In the name of God, the
light of holiness, who maketh the bright day
and the dark night. In the name of God, whose
being is infinite, before whom the heavens are,
as it were, but a pinch of dust; who brought
existence out of non-existence, and made innumerable happy worlds to revolve; from whose
dominion nothing is exempted; by whose providential care none is neglected. I will remember Him here in the beginning of my work; for
every beginning made with His remembrance

1 A

is blessed. By Him the ground of the heart is illuminated; He bloweth upon it the pure air of love; He poureth upon it the living water of knowledge. By Him a pen is made fruitful as a branch, a book resplendent as a beautiful garden, and words to bloom as odoriferous roses. With that remembrance alone will I fill the cup of my heart, and will sing new and entertaining stories.

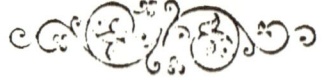

CHAPTER I.

————oo:o:oo————

On the birth of Prince Albert, his education, and arrival at mature years ; and his wish to marry Victoria.

There is a country of the world called Germany, the eminence of which is known everywhere. In its interior is a large district, called the Dukedom of Gotha, about 37 miles in area,* and containing about one hundred and fifty thousand inhabitants. The air of this district is pleasant, dry, and cool ; and the water refreshing and pure. The land is good, and very fertile, and every article of food and clothing is cheap there. In its neighbourhood is the city of Coburg, where the richest blessings of Providence display themselves, near which flows the river Itz, and where is a magnificent ducal Castle, having the appropriate name of Rosina, with a

* One German (square) mile is equal to 22 English miles.

garden entirely surrounding it. Here the birth of Albert took place; in this castle he made his entry into life on the 26th day of August in the Christian year 1819. The coming of Prince Albert into the world occasioned intense joy to his parents; but a few years after this the chain of their love became suddenly broken. Into the cup of unanimity dropped the deadly poison of separation.* The virtuous Louisa was separated from her husband, and passed all the rest of her life in loneliness. The Prince lived

---

* Duke Ernest of Saxe Coburg, one of the central states of Germany, had married Louisa, the highly accomplished and beautiful daughter of Augustus, Prince of Saxe-Gotha; of her, on the 26th August 1819, Prince Albert, the late husband of our august Queen, was born. Prince Albert's ancestors were warlike and energetic men. From the year A.D. 1455 they held the sovereignty and carried on the government of several states in the middle of Germany; and the Princes their descendants rule there to this day. After the birth of Prince Albert a disagreement by some means arose between his parents, in consequence of which his mother retired to a palace in Altenberg, and lived there apart from her husband till her death, which took place 30th August 1851. Some of Prince Albert's ancestors afforded powerful protection and assistance to Martin Luther, the man who set up the Protestant religion in opposition to the Roman Catholic, and who in consequence suffered much persecution.

in company with his elder brother, and used to divert himself with science and art. With study only he occupied his mind night and day; by study he made his heart to be wise, by study he learnt the secrets of the world, and his humble fortune expanded. He learnt so readily as to give his preceptor the greatest pleasure. One day he spoke to him thus with joy: "O Albert, virtuous, and of royal descent, to me thou seemest full of good fortune. With pains thou hast acquired thy present perfection; thy heart has obtained adornment corresponding to the beauty of thy face. Now, thy age has become quite mature, it is but natural that if a wise son like thee obtained a lady worthy of thee, royal by descent, and virtuous in behaviour, the garden of thy life would flourish, and, tasting the fruits of happiness, thou wouldst remain in the world ever glad; therefore, my accomplished pupil, this is the one hope of my soul, that thou make a hearty effort to be united to the worthy heiress of the Kingdom of England; and if thou do this, thou wilt not be disappointed. Procure through some one, the asking of this lady in marriage, or make thy desire known to thy father. Thou and she are near relations; you are two branches of one and the same tree; therefore lose no time in making these branches thoroughly one. The spring of thy virtuous youth is in its height; put in action therefore the effective dagger of contrivance; engraft speedily the plant of love; make soft the ground of thy heart with carefulness, bringing every good influence to bear upon it; tie the knot of union, for through this thou wilt taste fruits fresh and varied. From these, my words, learn thou the secret; and, having learnt it, lose not thy time, for if thou do, thou will be considered a fool. This youthful lady is suitable for thee, she is as it were the moon moving in the heavens.

When Albert heard words like these the passion of love arose in his heart; his face became, with blushes, like the flower of the pomegranate, the radiance of the fire of love shone upon it. Sleep, food, and study became distasteful to him; he lost repose; and the anxieties of love engrossed him. In the place of learning came distressing cares; his patience was consumed with the fire of impatience. From bashfulness he spoke not a single word, but merely looked downward, and maintained a respectful silence.

———◦◦º𝅘𝅥º◦◦———

Victoria's Portrait sent to Germany to Prince Albert.

The bearer of the portrait presented it to Prince Albert, and said*: If thy heart is anxious that thou shouldst see the bright face of Victoria, I can give thee now this picture, which, having seen, forget the distraction of thy heart. Consider thou this a present from thy beloved; by this keep up the remembrance of her, and thy love for her. Thee, a German Prince, I will cause to meet that Queen; I will contrive to heal the wound of thy loneliness. Thou wilt not find such a princess in the world, a lady on whom the moon bestows praises and congratulations. I am travelling in all the cities and towns of the world to find one perfectly good, in whom is nobility and pure ancestry, who

---

* In the year 1837, a hand-drawn portrait of Queen Victoria, by an eminent painter named Chalon, was sent as a present to Prince Albert.

possesses the jewel of pure religion, who has true love in his heart, and who knows how to gain the hand of a royal lady.

When Albert had heard these things, he set free his honeyed tongue and soft voice, and said : " O bearer of the portrait, may Providence keep thee in peace, for thou hast come here to-day like an angel, and hast given to me this best of news; thou hast administered the medicine for my secret pain. Thanks without number be to God that I have become acquainted with the condition of a lover. Rest thyself awhile, I will prepare a letter for Victoria; take it for me, and lay it at her feet; present it to her at an auspicious moment, and tell her all that thine eyes have seen."

—————○○¦○¦○○—————

Prince Albert writes Victoria a letter, acknowledging the Portrait presented to him, and informing her at the same time of his own grief and pain on account of his lonely condition.

O lady, greatly-beloved receive this my salutation as readily as thou inhalest the rosy fragrance of the morning; a salutation redolent with devotion to thee, whose praise shines bright as a flame. May it be welcome as the beautiful spring, under whose influence flowers, leaves, and withered trees come again into freshness; as the water, of life by which the world's verdure is maintained as life itself to the body, and as hope to any desponding one. Know thou that thy precious gift has reached me. I value it as the very life of my heart, the pearls of my eyes rest upon it, I see nought else anywhere. O bright eye of my soul! O protection of the happiness of all living things! O noblest foundation of universal justice! O splendid pillar of the temple of learning! O lady, eminent for the encouragement of art! I am thy faithful and devoted adorer. By the pain of separation from thee I am distressed; when I think upon thee I moan, with my head bent to the ground. How shall I make known to thee the sadness of my condition? When I would write thee a letter the water of my eyes flows from my pen instead of the black ink; my design therefore remains unaccomplished; blindness rests upon my eyes, and fire burns in my heart. In my feeling of love for

2 A

thee I am mad; I am a moth flying around a lighted candle. Could I but obtain a sight of thy lovely face I would never remove my eyes from off it. I am like an unsteady flickering candle of night; thou art like the dawning morning of sunshine. The lightning of love has fallen on the lantern of my body; and by the floods of those eyes it will never be quenched. As a moth flies about, then falls, flutters, and finally rests, so, unsteadily, does the lamp of my life burn. Were the black night of my grief to become ink, and with a pen of sighs my loneliness be described, yet would not the tale of my affliction be fully told. To a distressed heart there are a thousand anxieties, and every anxiety makes wounds without number. How then shall I apply ointment, and where healing plaster? For ten new wounds appear if one is healed. So fierce within me rages the fire of loneliness that though I swim always in a flood of tears, my body is burning to a cinder. May no soul experience the intense pain of separation! My anxiety to see thee, O dearly beloved one, is so great, that no description of it can be given;

my years glide by in expectancy; all my fancies revel in thy love. Thou appearest to me sometimes in my sleep, and my bed moves as though it had taken to itself the wings of flying birds. If thou ask as to thy place with me, I answer, by night the eyes, by day the heart; the door-keepers of those places being wakefulness and pain, which have the orders of the king of love. Though I have not seen thee I know thee. If thou hast understanding, thou wilt rightly estimate this pure love. Keep thy heart free from evil surmisings; I am one with thee in heart, though of a different country. To write more appears not good. Enjoy thou for ever a mighty Empire; may the civilized world remain subject to thy sway; may fame rest as a helmet upon thy head; may the great Giver be thy guide evermore. My heart is ready to make any sacrifice to ensure thy acceptance of me; my soul is under the foot of thy orders.

An Ode on seeing the Picture.

This thy picture fills me with indescribable pleasure :
A lovely rose set about with ringlets unnumbered.
The souls thou hast captured
Hang upon the arrows of thy eyelids,
And the talk of this goes on
Among the hunters of this universe.
Behold the streams of dropping blood in these my eyes !
They are like grains of rubies
Glittering from the midst of quicksilver.
Welcome, O nightingale, to go about this garden.
Talk O roses and tulips, talk about this fascinating one.
Hither has come the picture of a Jesus-like beloved one ;
And among all lifeless things the signs of life reappear.

When Victoria's mother heard concerning this matter from her daughter she was glad in heart with the hope of having a son-in-law like Albert, and replied thus : "O daughter, rash, and of little understanding, the object thou desirest is hard to attain. Albert, indeed, is greatly renowned; few men will be found like him in the world. He is born of a royal stock ; his pedigree is of the purest ; in heart he is religious ; he is learned, skilful, and clever ; he is indeed worthy of thee ; yet is there one great impediment. The hearts of the English people are intoxicated with haughtiness ; they despise a stranger and a foreigner ; they will not at all approve this thing, nor will they consider it honourable that thou shouldst be united in love to a child of Germany. Thou, the worthy heiress of the English throne, wilt be considered too high to be mated with a Prince of Germany. Albert, by his ancestors, is a pure German ; the English will not approve of thy marriage with him. But I will make every exertion for thee ; therefore let thy heart be patient and calm.

Prince Albert writes a letter to his father asking permission to marry Queen Victoria ; his father's reply thereto.

Albert thought he would acquaint his father with the true circumstances of his case, state his wishes, and ask his approval. He therefore applied his pen to paper. In the beginning he wrote the name of God, who makes the bright day and the black night, who is the benefactor of the world, and in whose hand is justice ; with whose goodness the whole world is filled ; with whom are the fears and the hopes of man ; who gives punishment to the wicked, and rewards to the righteous ; who is the God of heaven and the earth, the guide of hearts endued with goodness who brings prosperity and also desolation; who gives life to the withered and the weak; who blesses youth with bloom and fragrance, and who causes body and soul to droop in age; whose orders are obeyed over the whole earth; without whose permission not a fly can lift its wing in the air, nor an ant move its feet upon the ground; who from one pair filled the earth with people, and willed that nothing should ever be produced by a single one. No *one* in creation exists save God; for there is none worthy to be his equal. But all his productions in this world are from pairs; within the veil of this mystery all things are included. All time and space are filled with life; in man there is the light of love and knowledge. If in this world the species had not been in pairs, there would never have continued here a growing population. There is no divine religion in the world which does not allow of two becoming a pair. Wonderful is the law of development of the youth of the body. Without pairing the rosary of the body will not bud forth; through it love and friendship and kindness and fondness, the field of domestic happiness, flourishes. Vain is all worldly happiness without bodily gratification; the soul by itself cannot remain happy at all. Happy is the pair which has a child; wretched is the man who dies without one; the road to heaven is closed upon him, and in his lifetime he suffers shame and destitution. The name and memory of a father is perpetuated by a child; therefore without pairing, the world would become altogether desolate. The cause of all these words, this lengthy demonstration, is the wretched state of my heart. This world and this life have become to me insipid; my heart has gone, and songs, sport, and merriment have become poison to me; flowers, plants, and singing birds are all as nothing to me; he who has no heart feels everything vain. If thou art my father receive my complaint. My heart's love longs to be in the palace of Victoria; show me mercy then; oh, show me compassion! That lady has taken away my heart altogether. Whether people are great or small, high or low, they obtain happiness only by marriage; this is the general experience of the world; and religion and even learned men make no objection thereto.

Thou art wise and prudent, and discerning, there is no need of writing more to thee. The blood of my heart drops like water through the avenues of my eyes; but notwithstanding this intense grief, and this overwhelming distress, I crave thy command. What is thy wish? What are thy thoughts towards me?

—◦◦⁝◦⁝◦◦—

Victoria's mother writes a letter to her (own) brother, who was Prince Albert's father, and consults him on the subject of Victoria's betrothal, and other matters.

As soon as Victoria's mother understood the cause of her daughter's unhappiness, she wrote to her brother on that subject. First she blessed God, from whom are the springs of existence and non-existence, whose servants are we all in this world. And then she proceeded thus: " Toil and care and bliss and splendour, are continually passing over the head of man; what need therefore for me to descant at all upon matters such as these. But a difficulty has come in my way, the solution of which I seek in thy counsel; therefore ask I advice of thee, my wise-hearted brother. I have nourished a plant in the field of love, and have watered it with care all my life long. In-

stead of manure I bestowed on my plant attention and knowledge; I caused it to grow, and be
beautiful, and to improve day by day. By toiling
day and night, through frost, and cold, and heat,
I developed it into a fruitery, rich, and exalted
on high; and I expected to taste delicious fruits
from off it. But suddenly I saw the effect of
the influence of time upon it; that time had withered its leaves and fruit, and burnt its branches;
that the fragrance of happiness had fled, and
the evil odour of grief had taken its place; that
my plant, my daughter, had become filled with
grief, by reason of her love for thy son. Albert
has secretly thrown a net over her, and in his
net her soul has become a prey. I have employed
many devices, and have spoken many words, yet
no good appears effected. Therefore O brother
point out to me a remedy, for none occurs to me
except that my daughter and thy son may spend
their lives in everlasting love. The auspicious
union of Victoria and Albert may create new
hopes in the world, may sow abundant seeds in
the field of time, and give life to the royal family
of England."

3 \

Prince Albert's father talks with Albert concerning the letter which he had written to him; and afterwards having received the letter of the Duchess, goes with his son and his whole family to London.

Albert's father read the letter he had sent, and thoroughly weighed its contents; he felt no compassion for his son, but commanded to call him at once. He then addressed him in anger, with words harsh and cold, saying, O son, rash and of little sense, that thou dost entertain such foolish thoughts, thou hast abandoned happiness, and art taking on thy head trouble and grief. What is love? what is friendship? and what is this commotion in thy breast? Foolish boy, heretofore engrossed in eating, drinking, and learning. Where didst thou get this information, and these notions? Where didst thou see any one to love? Where didst thou lose thy heart? Why dost thou prate thus? And who made thee prate? Hath Satan caused thee to go astray? Whence canst thou, an inhabitant of the city of Gotha, and a mere Duke's son, have obtained such a thought or notion as that there should be a connection between thy heart's love and the great heiress of the throne of England. What need hath she of one like thee ? She is the moon in the high heavens, thou a mere atom on the earth ; she a cypress of paradise, thou a reed of the desert; she a nightingale of the garden, thou an insect of the grass. A nation proud and haughty like the English will think thee thoroughly mad. O son consider well, and do not plunge into the whirlpool of calamity. The jewel of thy expectation will never come into thy hands. Talk to me now in a becoming manner ; display not rudeness and shamelessness, for he who pains the heart of his father is an evil son ; he who abandons the customs of his father is a vicious son. He only is a true son who makes glad his father's heart ; he only is a true son who holds to his father's name; he only is a true son who obeys his father's commands.

Having heard this Albert felt greatly grieved, and scalding water filled the two narcissus flowers,—his eyes. He despaired of life, his face became pale, his lips dry, and his breath cold. Then, having looked downwards, he turned his face away, for he was sore vexed by the words of his father.

When the letter of the Duchess arrived, the Prince's father read it, and understood the whole matter. He came to know the grief that was upon his son, and was much afflicted, on account of past occurences. He bestowed upon it careful attention, and finally it appeared to him good; for if one like Victoria became his daughter-in-law, he would attain to much worldly distinction. His head would reach the heavens through his greatness, and his descendants would continue flourishing and happy. Through a daughter-in-law, so highly favoured by fortune as Victoria, his interest and influence in the world would increase. He became so glad at heart that the intensity of his gladness was sufficient to resuscitate the body of a dead man, or to make the old bloom with youth again, for he considered himself at the height of good fortune. Then he called Albert and spoke with him kindly words of wisdom, saying : " O Son, thou seemest truly fortunate, difficulties of every sort are suddenly removed far away. The desire of thy soul is accomplished. Be glad at heart and wise in mind; give thanks to the Lord for his mercies, for the

visible and the hidden are known unto him.
Through his providential care the earth is always fresh, myriads upon myriads of creatures
live by him. Through his loving kindness man
is supremely happy ; by his mercy the world re-
volves and time runs on ; from him are life and
death and goodness. We are all his servants.
Trust thou in Him for every thing. Let not
greatness make thy heart proud. All pride
shall utterly fall to the ground ; the greatness
of no earthly thing will continue.

Now thou hast to form friendship with a
foreign people, maintain my name, my character,
and my reputation. Never forget the country of
thy birth, show kindness to the weak and the
needy. Study thou the peculiar disposition of the
English, for there is in their constitution a
natural haughtiness. Let thy speech on every
subject be suited to the time. We must now
go to England, where thou wilt meet thy beloved; therefore from to-day prepare thyself; read
this good news from thy aunt (father's sister)
and write thou a befitting answer thereto. We
shall surely proceed there soon.

Then Albert made this reply : O, wise father, highly favoured by fortune ! Nature has bestowed on thee perfect understanding. From thy precepts the light of my knowledge is derived. The dust of thy feet forms my pillow. I obey thy commands as I obey the mandates of religion. In this world a son has honour only from the father. May no grief ever betide thee ; may no evil eye ever rest upon thee ; may thy ill wishers be overthrown in their wickedness ; may thou continue in the world, in the full enjoyment of happiness.

The Duke now gave an order to make ready all things necessary for the journey, and without delay they travelled stage after stage, now by land, now by water. In the Christian year 1836 this happy event took place. All arrived at the port of London. The news of their arrival soon reached the Duchess, whereupon she made the necessary arrangements to afford accommodation of every kind to her guests, and Victoria immediately went upon the terrace. Like the shining full moon in the heavens, did that beautiful beloved one stand, and like a gazelle casting forward her mild and longing eye, she saw her thoughtful lover walking with gracefulness—the good and renowned prince of Gotha. Having come near, she opened her ruby-coloured lips thus:"Wonderful art thou, O Prince, truly wonderful. It is well that thou art come. Thy face glows with brightness like the sun. May the Lord of both the worlds bestow his blessing upon thee. May He give thee thy heart's desire. Thou hast troubled to come to this place; by thy face the black night of sorrow has been turned into bright and joyful day. The fragrance of thy body has pervaded this city; the roses of the garden have forgotten their odour.*

---

* In this work, on every suitable occasion, the words *rose* (that is the *flower* of the rose tree) and *nightingale* will very often occur; but in this country the colour and odour of this flower and the voice of the singing of this bird do not seem to be worth admiring, therefore perhaps some ignorant reader might judge less favourably of them. Hence we might quote the words of the eminent authors, Sir H. Rawlinson, Sir R. K. Porter, and Sir William Jones, about the rose and nightingale of Persia, and from this the reader will be convinced that the flower and this bird exist in our ancient country of Persia, and are considered worthy of great admiration. Besides this, other authors mention that even in the earth about the roots of the rose tree of Persia there exists so much odour that many people at the time of bathing or washing their hands and feet rub that earth upon their bodies as soap.

When Albert heard these sweet words he saw the face before him like the lustre of the sun. In appearance it resembled the light of the dawn. Even the dust, through her brightness, shone like rubies. He answered, O lady of pleasing countenance, may thou be happy and may the Lord show thee favour. I was desirous only to see thy face; in the night lying down, I counted the stars; by day, feeling restless and disquieted I was continually crying in the court of the Lord, that He, the God of mercy and fulfiller of one's desires, might show me thy lovely face. Now I render him thanks without number, because at length he hath shown me thy face, lovely as the pomegranate flower. Cause me to hear thy heart-charming voice, thy sweet speech, and to see thy gracefulness and elegance.

Having heard this, Victoria became exceeding glad, and walked in the garden with Albert. While walking a voice was heard to say, Rejoice O garden, O leaves and trees rejoice, for the best-beloved has come to perambulate in this place. O happy spot, O happy day! the thorns have bloomed into gaily coloured flowers; on all sides, flowers and fruits send forth a rose-like fragrance. All flowers lift up their golden cups, and dew fills them with variously coloured wine. The breeze wafts the fragrance far from hence; all objects in this garden unite to leap for joy. All the trees are lifting their branches on high invoking the Lord; they are worshippers before Him, because abundance of pleasures and delight has come here; from a distant country the renowned best-beloved has come. Arise O gardener, arise quickly, and come; bring wreaths of champa and jasmine; sing O nightingales a strain of pleasant song, that the beloved of my soul may be cheered, that the owner of the garden may be delighted.

Words spoken by a lover in the pleasant interview with the beloved.

STANZA I.

I bestow on the person of my beloved the jewel of my soul,
What better use can I make of this jewel by keeping it?
Congratulations to thee, O weak heart,
That a virtuous lover *of Jesus-like spirit*,
Has come hither and walks in this place,
Like the spring of *the garden of Paradise.*
Rejoice ye fruits for the morning breeze is blowing,
And nightingales are singing merrily songs and lays,
And strains of exquisite beauty.

STANZA 2.

O ye leaves and trees, sing in David-like strains instructive
    songs ;
For the Solomon of the city of Gotha,
Has sown love in the place of my heart.
Stand in awe ye cypresses, stand in awe,
For the dove has suddenly come,
And with a branch of the flower of love,
Has gained a victory over the nightingale.
Like the pillars of an arch,
The walls and gates of this palace
Flung wide their arms when the beloved came rushing
    alone.

STANZA 3.

Come my beloved, sit by me,
Take off thy (travelling) garments and be at ease ;
Thou hast been tossed about with the toils of thy journey,
Take rest and refresh thyself.
The pearls of dew dropping from thy forehead,
Are like grains of diamonds falling from the clouds ;
O man of a pleasing and beautiful countenance,
By these thy glowing cheeks,
A thal † of dazzling brightness has been bound
On the face of the moon.

STANZA 4.

So wonderfully lustrous has heaven formed thy face,
That the atmosphere is bathed in the ocean of its brilliancy;
A messenger came and told me
That a Joseph-like lover arrived.

---

* Thal થાળ a round vessel used usually as a plate, which is kept
scrupulously bright and polished.—*Translator's note.*

With Zuleika like heart I rose at once
To see thy countenance.
This Micerian soul is an offering at thy feet.
Without thee the garden of my happiness
Was as it were a Canaan of grief.

(*Reply of the beloved.*)

STANZA 1.

The black night of distressing grief
Has become bright by meeting thee,
Near the corpse of my dead heart, as it were,
A light of life has come.
Thou speakest with such grave fascination,
As to steal in a moment,
The life-long devotion of a virtuous-hearted lover.

STANZA 2.

What description shall I give of this face and this heart ?
Running swifter than fast-flowing tears,
And hotter than deep drawn sighs,
I have brought to thee this soul,
Which with tenderest care
I have nourished and brought up ;
I now commit that soul to thee.
With great delight I stand here in thy abode, O beloved,
At last the Righteous Lord has accomplished
The work according to my desire.

STANZA 3.

I am ready to bow to whatever thou,
Heart charmer, mightst do ;
Whether thou woundest me with rage,
Or fillest my heart with love.
I am not so base a man as to say
One thing with one mouth,
And belie it afterward.

If I were to swerve from thee here
Divine wrath would overtake me.
O beloved, may thou live in honour, renown, and joy;
May the merciful Father of both the worlds
Shield thee from every danger.

STANZA 4.

To the very last moment thou wast a guest
In the chamber of my heart.
Now having seen thee with the eye,
I am ready to offer my soul.
After the blackness of intense grief,
Appeared the moon of thy face,
Through joy at this happy event
My head has reached the highest heaven.
The treasure for which I longed anxiously for years
Stands now before my face;
Rejoice, O my soul and be glad!

Then they parted each from the other, and severally joined the magnificent assembly gathered in the palace of Windsor. In the same palace was their abode. The Duchess of Kent discharged the duty of supplying all the wants of the guests. She showed hospitality to her brother in every way. Victoria also was anxiously attentive, and taking every trouble, busied herself both body and mind, attending to the guests day and night, and making them happy with her cheerful countenance, so that they spent many days with pleasure and delight, in the enjoyment of singing, in social meetings, and parties of various kinds; in love meetings, and every agreeable and heart-exciting occupation. The Duchess made all arrangements with her brother and bestowed Albert's name on Victoria (betrothed her to him). They postponed the marriage to a distant date, saying when the lady shall be formally crowned we will complete all the ceremonies of marriage, we will do all things according to the practice of the country and of our religion. After this the Duke prepared for his homeward journey, and caused all things required on the way to be in readiness, that he might leave for his own country.

Words spoken on the eve of a lover's departure to his own country.

When my lover prepares for his journey,
What shall I do?
Shall I devise an antidote for separation?
Or shall I resign life altogether?
Coming suddenly, he caused the lightning
Of dear love to flash upon my heart,
My heart has been scorched into kabab,
What shall I do?

He is going, oh he is going,
The spring of the garden of this body,
He is going, as the precious soul
From the body.
Not a flower has been plucked
From the garden of our meeting,
Yet he goes away ;
In the wilderness of separation,
The tiger is making a prey of my heart.

Parting from my lover will deprive me,
Of my pride and happiness,
Useless is the ring when the diamond is gone,
And how can its cost be redeemed ?
If all the adornments of the soul go with the lover,
Why should the body remain ?
The hope of the world goes from my heart,
On whom then shall I bestow attention ?

Having filled his eyes with desperation,
He flies away like a deer.
With the arrows of the rays of those eyes
The heart of many a soul is pierced.
Like the flashing of the lightning
In a fiery chariot flies he away,
By his rapid rushing moving,
The electric currents of the earth are put to shame.

Separation from my own soul
Is easier to endure,
Than banishment from thy face ;
In the strict interchange of love,
I am the body, thou the soul.
Having come late and sat for a moment,
Thou hast robbed me of my peace.
Having cast me into the mire of separation,
Thou hast gone to thy fatherland.

This night separation from my beloved
Gives me warning of death.
The grief of this death knows no night,
It is the storm foreboding the judgment day.
Blood runs down from my eyes,
My soul is severed from the body,
Come quickly back again,
For thou only art my rest and bliss.

Last night that shining moon
Took leave of me and went away,
My heart's sighs blessed him,
And my tears accompanied him.
Like prosperity came he slowly,
Like adversity carried he joy away quickly.
He, like the life of the body,
Having gone out once, never came back again.

Like the kernel in the midst of an almond,
That man of fascinating countenance
Departed, leaving in the recesses of my heart
A void completely desolate.
As a wicked man at the time of his death
Improves his morals and faith,
So didst thou when going on thy journey,
Make to me new vows and promises.

Thou art going from my sight,
But the mark of grief will be left in my heart.
Having come hither like a firefly,
Thou hast burned the flower garden of my soul.
Thou camest tardily, as hope to the hopeless ;
Thou departest as the favour
Of a hard-hearted friend.

CHAPTER II.

Prince Albert arrives at his own country and completes his studies. Victoria ascends the throne, and the prince thereupon projects another visit to England.

ALBERT at once embarked in a vessel: a splendid gift was placed in the arms of the sea. That moon of love sat in a ship, and drew along as it were the whole illuminated waters. He reached his country in safety with his father, and engaged in studies of every kind. He associated with the wise and learned, and studied every subject with eagerness. He perplexed his tutors with inquiries, and by earnest application he attained wonderful proficiency; in the society of the learned he became himself learned, and acquired profound knowledge of the laws of religion and of the state. He travelled in all cities and countries, and obtained all the knowledge requisite for a king. When the

year 1840 arrived Queen Victoria had been
seated securely on the throne, had placed upon
her head the God-shadowed crown, and had
become superior in majesty to all others in the
world. The canopy of justice overspread the
earth, the hearts of the wicked melted with fear,
food and profitable industry became abundant
in the earth ; by the bright drops of the cloud
of benevolence the whole world became a flourishing garden. Never was such a flower seen
in the spring time, never was such a lark
brought up in a nest. From the court of heaven
such strict justice descended, that the hearts
of all people were happy and glad. The tree of
prosperity was firmly rooted, and gave the nation
most delicious fruits to eat. The neck of oppression was cut off by the sword of justice.
The rights of the weak and the strong were
made equal, the water of the stream of justice
flowed through the world, and the earth became
beautiful and green with the verdure of happiness. The shadow of impartiality spread
itself abroad, and restrained the hands of devils
from evil.

5

ODE.

In praise of Victoria.

Many many thanks to God,
That from the royal seed of the English nation
Came forth this incomparably precious pearl.
From the royal nest soared aloft this Homa,
Out of the galaxy of famous ones this star appeared.
No rosary could show so beautiful a rose as this,
No tulip garden could produce a tulip such as this.
The hearts of all people were delighted
That at length the Lord had heard their prayer.
The heart-charming spring of mercy
Bloomed forth, and a dead world lived again.
The Lady who sits upon the throne,
Is a Queen of a pure heart,
A light in darkness to all grieved ones,
A giver of hope to the hopeless,
The idol of the hearts of the religious,
The dread of unjust kings.
A good and renowned Queen enthroned
In the hearts of her subjects,
She is the bright reflection of divine love,
Well fitted for the crown and the throne.
The sure support of religion and justice:
In whom rests the confidence of the world.
May thy years, the incidents of thy life,
Thy wealth, thy condition,
Thy family, thy descendants, thy fortune, thy throne,
Remain secure in this world,
From generation to generation ;
May thy years be happy,
The incidents of thy life propitious,
Thy wealth increasing, thy condition blessed.
May thy family prosper, thy descendants endure,
Thy throne be firm, thy fortune subservient to thy will.

A little time after this occurrence the Queen again remembered Albert; she caused a letter, official, and according to rule, to be written to his father.*

When the letter reached Albert's father he was filled with exceeding joy. He instantly called Albert, and spoke to that fortunate one thus : O, handsome son of rare fortune, my miserable day has become happy through thee. A branch of the tree by whose virtue wealth has penetrated into the depths of the earth has come into thy hand; whose feet this rolling earth kisses, and on whom the kings of the earth bestow their praises. By this my soul is so much gladdened that, though old, I have become young again. Then Albert gave answer thus: O honoured

* "On the 15th December 1839 Viscount Torrington and Colonel Grey, two great officers of state, were sent with suitable presents by the English Government per steamer *Fearless* to Germany, to meet Prince Albert, on behalf of the English Government ; and having conferred a title on him in the name of the Government, to bring him and his whole family to London ; accordingly, on the 24th January, these officers bestowed the title on the Prince with great pomp in the city of Gotha, and on the 28th January they and Albert's family embarked for England."

father of a noble stock : to thy great virtue all this is owing. I rejoice in a good father like thee ; the dust of thy feet is the support of my body ; thy approbation is the adornment of my soul ; thy commands are the duties of my life.

Albert's father prepared himself at once, taking necessary provisions, furniture, and money. Having sat in a boat Prince Albert went forward accompanied by his family. The gallant vessel floated down the stream, and did not leave her track on the way.*

From a distance she appeared like an alligator, or like the moon of the second day (day after new) sailing through the heavens, or like a tree growing in the midst of deep waters, casting its shadow as it moved in a hundred directions ; or she was like a horse leaping without feet and bound only to the surface of the water ; so swift and so lofty of mien that the sun from afar uttered a shout of approbation. As a lover

---

* On the 28th January 1840 Prince Albert (with his father and relations) set out to go to London ; he wept bitterly at parting from his own palace of Ehrenberg, as well as from his own dear country.

weeps on account of separation from his beloved, so the ship beating her breast, filled her skirts with water. She sometimes appeared from her motion tired and weary, and the bubbles about her seemed like blisters on the feet. In body she was a strong negress, but in speed lively; in her womb were hundreds of children, yet did she never bear. So swiftly by a succession of graceful leaps did she move, that the waters flowed gushingly behind her. Her deportment was like that of a holy man, who without hands and feet (being without wealth and devoted to piety) lives upon water, continually spreading the carpet of prayer, and bowing her head to kiss the book of the sea. When the sea desired to sing its praise, the tongue of the waves uttered sublime songs. Riding along Albert saw the bubbles and waves on the watery plain, reminding him of the ball and chogan.*

From whichever side the vessel turned her head the waters of the sea would retire; they moved from their place giving way on all sides

---

* Chogan " is a game like cricket, played on horseback.

as for the great Zoroaster when he passed through the water "Darati."

When Albert saw the foam of the channel a feeling of delight arose in his heart, and he said, O righteous God, how exceedingly pure is the water of this sea, that its bubbles appear like starry eyes in which can be seen the forms of swimming fishes. If shells be here pearls may be counted, its waves appear to extend hundreds of furlongs. Strong it is, as if filled with uncontrollable madness, its waves are like the raging of an infuriated elephant, their crests appear like alligators, before them the roaring of lions would be nothing. In the eyes of the fishes shine the fire of light, and on every wave are hundreds of lamps. Deriving pleasures and enjoyments from reflections such as these, all the travellers went on, and reached the port of London in safety, and the vessel anchored in the Thames.

CHAPTER III.

———o·o·o·o·o———

Prince Albert, with his father and all his family, having come
    to London, and reached Victoria's Palace, performs
    the auspicious ceremony of marriage, and gives an
    entertainment.

THEN they all bent their steps toward the
City, and the news of their coming speedily
reaching the palace, Victoria came out, attended
by her maids, having in their hands bouquets
of flowers. These in their joy they scattered
upon the bridegroom, and having shouted welcome, inquired of his health. The meeting was
a joyous and delightful one, gladness reigned
every where. Several days passed and preparations for the marriage were completed, and the
ministers and the people, the wise and the
thoughtful, fixed unanimously on one particular
day, and at noon of the auspicious 10th day of the
fortunate second month, the necessary ceremony

took place. All was done according to the rites of religion, and the customs of the country, and the virtuous Victoria was united with Albert. In an august and magnificent assembly a covenant was entered into to this effect :—

I, Albert, son of the Gotha prince, resign myself to thy will from this day ; with the sign of this ring I now wed thee, and I will live with thee from this day for ever. I will not be wanting in the duty of a husband, in all purity, kindness, and faithfulness ; I will not permit my love to fail thee even for a moment. Should I do so with thee, may God do even so with me. Having seen with my eyes, assented with my understanding, and having solemnly vowed this according to the customs of this country and of the Church, I swear it. Moreover in my full age I have entered into this engagement ; and have in this promised that the desire of another shall never be entertained by me.

Then Victoria spoke such words as these :—

Thou art my husband and I thy wife ; from now to the last of my days, with thee only will I continue united in body and soul, in poverty or in riches, in prosperity or in adversity ; thy will and thy law will I keep, thy lawful behests will I obey with all my heart, and will remain submissive to thy virtuous wishes.

Having completed these ceremonies, and this covenant, the sun found rest in the arms of the moon, for Albert became Victoria's husband. From every quarter arose a shout of gladness, the whole assembly tendered their congratulations, and all earnestly desired their welfare.* Then came Victoria's honoured mother: she first turned her face towards the bright sky; then having invoked a blessing, uttered these words :—

O good daughter, O wise prince; only to day have I found any true delight in the world, for before my death I have seen this auspicious event, by which the glory of England will be maintained. May the Protector of the World, holy and exalted, in His mercy prolong your lives. Dwelling in harmony may you experience unbounded happiness, and keep your hearts set on God's laws.

Then came other ladies near, their royal apparel glittering with gold, from whose persons

---

* On the 10th February 1840 Albert and Victoria were married in the royal chapel of St. James. The kings and princes of many countries had asked Victoria in marriage, but all in England with one mind approved Albert, and for his expenses they voted him an income of Rs. 3,00,000.

6

issued forth the smell of perfumes, all hearts
rejoicing, all tongues sweet; they invoked
blessings, and spoke—

O Khosru of Germany—O Shirin of England,
may you taste delicious draughts of the honey
of love, may you continue in this world steadfast in true affection. May you have many
sons, and thus establish the throne; may you be
happy in body and mind by seeing the happiness
of your children; by virtuous actions may your
state be ever prosperous, and may the hearts of
your subjects be ever set upon you.

When these blessings and ceremonies were
finished in joy and gladness, the voice of tri-
umph arose from every side, with guns, and bells,
and bands of music; in every house, too, arose
the heart-charming sounds of cornets, flutes,
harps, pianos, and singing of various sorts; cannon
boomed from every fort—one making a whirring
noise, another a noise like thunder; their
smoke flew high and far away, blinding the
eyes of hostile men. On the face of the firmament set the clouds of jealousy, and the atmos-
pheric space was filled with echoings. The ships

and boats in the river were decorated and appeared splendid. Flags flaunted in the air far and near, and in the whole of London was seen only the light of joy. When the king of night came majestically along, he brought with him an innumerable array of dazzling roses, filled the expanse of the heavens with stars, and sprinkled upon the garden of the world gems of brilliancy. The lamps upon the vessels in the river appeared like small stars of the firmament, and by their reflection the surface of the river appeared burning like the fire of Ravan Lanká; * or as sparkling rubies embroidered upon a ground of silver, so did the lamps appear upon the bosom of the water; and the bubbles, by the light of the lamps, appeared like golden fruits in crystal glasses. So pure became the waters of the Thames that one could see in them the image even of the soul of his body. It was not a river, but as it were a flower garden; and the bodies of the fishes glittered like rose leaves. Every

* The great fire which burnt up Ceylon (anciently called Lanká), in the war between Rama and Ravan, celebrated in the great poem Ramayana.

where were clusters of variously decked boats;
the vessels were as shaking mountains, which
made graceful motions like peacocks coquetting
in the garden of Paradise.

An assembly met as in the garden of heaven.
The bounties of God were prepared in an elegant
manner; kings and princes and chiefs met together; fairy-faced ladies and royal dames assembled in costly garments. Candles and lamps
dazzled the eye, and a handsome table with
delicious viands was laid out, food tasty and
fragrant was served, and confections and fruits
of various sorts.

(The praise of the Assembly.)

Many an assembly must have met in the
world, but one so orderly, so grand as this, there
never could have been. Such fragrant scent
went forth from it, as if the dew of *atar* had
fallen from heaven. The air became fragrant
as the musk-chamber of the (musk) deer, the
hangings being of the cloth of Tartary and China.
Such was the exuberance of joy pervading that

place, that the dry strings of the guitar became resplendent.

· Through the lamps the night became bright as the day, by the brightness of their moons, a veil was, as it were, thrown over the moon of the heavens; so much light rose from all these lamps that a glittering came forth from the black feathers of the crow; such magnificent chandeliers were hanging there that they seemed to be clusters of glassy flowers in a garden of light, in which the dazzling jets of flame appeared like ripe fruits on the trees of Paradise. As in the firmament there is a display of jewels, so the spectacle presented here was a brocade of pearls. The lights shone out in the palace with such splendour that the stars painted their eyes with *surma.** The light shining in that palace was

---

* Surma means the sulphuret of antimony.

There are two explanations of this figure; (1) the light of the lamps was so dazzling, that the eyes of the stars could not endure it, so it became necessary to strengthen them by painting them with surma.

(2) The light of those lamps appeared so pleasant to the stars in the firmament that they took, as it were, the smoke going forth from those lamps and adorned their eyes by painting them with it.

like the light of heaven, and the ground was fully sown with joy; every corner appeared abounding with pleasant fruits, and the field of the heart blooming under the influence of the essence of the wine.

(About Musical Instruments.)

When the reign of wine (the time during which wine was drunk) was finished, from every side arose the sound of musical instruments. The strings of the *Tumbora* awoke from their sleep, and the hands of the players moved very gracefully. The Tabla appeared like scales and weights in which playing and singing were equally balanced. The gourd-bodied, heart-charming (three string) guitar became a swimmer in the sea of delightful singing. Accordians soothed every heart, and violins and flageolets played so deliciously as to affect the senses like the well known scent distilled from the veins of the leaves of roses. The wires of the rebeck appeared dry, yet made they the water

of life flow in every one. Trombones sounded
so impressively that letters were imprinted
upon the face of the air. Such arrows went forth
from the bows of the guitars that the hearts of
young and old were pierced. All griefs found
themselves dispersed under the influence of
the violins, the cornets destroyed complicated
difficulties, the flutes sent forth such warm
breath that hearts hard as ice were softened,
and as sheaves shed ripe grains, so did distracted lovers send forth sighs from their hearts.
Outwardly the body of the flute appeared old
and unattractive, without hands or feet, at-
tenuated and blind, but such wonderful secrets
were within it that like the rod of Musa it
removed affliction far away.* Its body was not
longer than a span, but there were in it the
depths of the sea of music. The charm of its
breath penetrated every ear, it became a lamp to
the seeing and a rod to the blind. In its bowels

* Musa was a Jewish prophet whom the English call
Moses. The greatest wonder about him was this, that, keeping in his hand an *Aso* or small rod, every thing the rod
touched turned, it is said, to what was desired.

there were soul-charming strains, as the child
Jesus in the womb of Mariam. *

In praise of Dancing.

The cypress statured ladies danced like peacocks, which made tumults to arise in the hearts
of lovers.   On their fairy formed heads glittered
pearls, at the sight of which the sea of love in
every heart became agitated.   The graceful motions of the hands of the dancers confused the
eyes of all men who observed them.   When they
turned their steps one after another, all the
senses of a man fell beneath their feet.   What
shall I say of the Mendozas and Polkas ?
for the philosophic and the pious lost their
peace of mind through them; observing the
dancers' motions, the moon forgot her own; and

* Here the allusion is as follows :—Mariam is the mother
of Christ, the prophet of Christians, and as this woman, according to the faith of these people, becoming pregnant by Divine
power, without carnal knowledge of man, gave birth to so
eminent and benevolent a son as Christ, so as it were from the
bowels of the flute pleasant sounds issued, which soothed the
hearts of the grieved and afflicted, and bestowed upon them
rest and joy.

their gracefulness made the face of Venus blush. The Polka was kept up with such zest and excitement that there was a stir among the angels of heaven. Every twisted hair of the ringlets on their heads brought upon hundreds of souls harassing troubles. In every direction the arrows of their eyes were flying, by which the old and the young were wounded. In short the ball was gracefulness itself, which made the stars bite their own bodies with jealousy; by such performances men's senses and patience were stolen, and at every step their innermost heart was drawn away. When the beautiful ones arose again for the Quadrille, the high heaven bent low to see them; yea all the revolving planets stood still majestically, as if the day of judgment had taken its birth from the womb of eternity. When the performance of singing and dancing reached its climax, the dead rose up from the ground superlatively enamoured of it. Such radiance came from the bodies of the dancers that the very lamps put their hands over their eyes. By the innumerable attractions and elegant manners displayed by the ladies the

7 A

core of the heart and of austerity (religious feeling) were stolen. No signs were made but greatly captivated, no glances cast but were the deepest spells; it was less like a ball than the assembly of hundreds of Jesus-like glorified ones at the day of judgment. At the tripping of the footsteps along the floor, the gravity of the spectators' patience, even though it were firm as a mountain, was completely rooted out. As pollen drops from the anthers of roses, so did colour leave the faces and self-possession the brains of those who saw the dancers. When they raised their eyes, making graceful motions, the stars hid their brightness within a veil. When they moved their eyebrows making any sign, the beautiful face of the moon became pale; when they turned their radiant countenances towards the east, the sun fled and plunged into the west.

(In praise of Singing.)

When the heart-charming singer was ready, the whole assembly cried out, Sing, O singer, sing new songs, for love deliciously sweet has touched the heart. Take great pains to amuse us, at this pleasant time, for some souls are still held in the grief of loveliness; strive, be compassionate, perform wondrous deeds, like Jesus. Make these soul-less bodies revive; with persuasive arts, with graceful manners, do thou delight them; cause them to drink honey, shower upon them sweetness, and cause all bitterness to pass away. Then the singer took hearty encouragement, and began her graceful and captivating performances. By the influence of the tune a glow was brought even upon sun-like faces, playing most enchanting music on the accordian, the minstrel made the altars of the heart fragrant with love; breathing through her ruddy lips into the plaintive flute, she soothed the anxieties and griefs of the hearts of all, and from her charming mouth she drew forth such delicious strains as to cause drops of joy to flow from their eyes like cataracts; and singing the airs of her songs with pathos she made the sensations of love descend into the hearts of half dead men. Singing may be likened to a wonderful tree which brings forth varieties of fruit with amazing speed. Under its shades are the joys of both the worlds, and in its very root is the honey of love.

When all this merriment and joy, lasting through the night, was finished, and the dawn of the morning had come, the bridegroom and the bride retired to their private apartments.

———✦———

(Words of a lover on the occasion of meeting his beloved.)

> O life of my soul, O life of my soul, ⎱
> O life of my soul, O life of my soul. ⎰ Chorus.

He who in mercy has placed
The beautiful rose in the arms of the thorn,
Has at last given to my arms,
The neck of thy body.

   (O life of my soul, &c.)

The moth on whose heart
The lightning of love had fallen,
Has at last found a bright flame
In the lantern of thy embraces.

   (O life &c.)

Truly those are blessed moments
When my eyes rest upon thy face,
For thy countenance soothes my wounds, and heals them.

   (O life &c.)

Separation from thee has made
My fate dark and dismal;
But blessed be patience,
Which has supported me till now.

(O life &c.)

I wept so much on account of separation from thee,
That my weeping made a cleft in the stones.
And I indeed must have been harder than a stone
To be alive to this day.

(O life &c.)

Death having considered me dead
Has many a time gone away from me;
And indeed it made no mistake,
For a lonely lover seldom lives.

(O life &c.)

Grief threw such poison
Upon the threshold of my soul's abode,
That death, knowing its bitterness,
Would not enter the house of this body.

(O life &c.)

How shall I describe my feeling of love for thee !
I burnt as fire in my loneliness,
By that very fire which keeps
The lamp of to-night so bright, was my body scorched.

(O life &c.)

When I asked the physicians for a remedy,
They answered me thus in despair:
Drink thou as sherbet night and day,
The blood of thy heart and the water of thine eyes.

(O life &c.)

If any one wish to learn the character of love,
Let him learn from me ;
Burning, weeping, brooding by day,
And wakefulness by night.

(O life &c.)

As a thief watches at night,
So would sleep watch near my tearful eyes ;
But when it saw my sad heart wakeful,
It turned away despairingly.

(O life &c.)

Innumerable thanks to God,
That my lips have met thy lips in joy ;
O heart-charming maid,
I now commit to thee the soul which came to my lips.

(O life &c.)

By uniting with thee,
The past years of my life have returned ;
Having seen thy Jesus-like beautiful countenance,
The spring of my soul is blooming afresh.

(O life &c.)

(*Reply of the beloved.*)

Chorus. What canst thou know of my condition !
　　　　Thou hast lived far from me ;
　　　　The distress I felt is known to God alone.

Without thee, O heart-charming lover,
My eyes had ever continued
Red as the tulip of Shirin,
And filled with the water of grief.

(What canst, &c.)

Like the drowsy eyes of king Khusru,
My fortune was in a pleasant sleep,
Or like the body of Maznoon,
My mind was not enjoying full consciousness.

(What canst, &c.)

Or like the ringlets of Leli,
My state was incomprehensible,
And the more I called thee to remembrance
The more my distress increased.

(What canst, &c.)

As the bodies of pomegranate grains
Are pricked by the stones in the midst of them,
So by the arrow-like points of drops of blood
This body was tormented.*

(What canst, &c.)

From the time when my love for thee
Pierced like a thorn the foot of my heart,
The youthfulness of my body withered,
And my soul burnt in the fire of grief.

(What canst, &c.)

---

* When Prince Albert came to London for the first time he danced at many balls and parties with Queen Victoria, but the Queen did not for some time find a good opportunity for giving him a token of her favour; on a certain occasion, however, when a ball was given to a large party in the royal palace, and Victoria had danced with Albert with great zest and enjoyment, she placed in his hands elegantly and gracefully at parting a beautiful bouquet of flowers, which Prince Albert took with great affection and gratitude, and tried to fix it in some part of his dress, but having a suit in which there was no place for it, he instantly took his knife from his pocket and cut the cloth near his heart and fixed the bouquet there, to the delight of his renowned beloved one, and the surprise of the whole assembly.

CHAPTER IV.

Victoria bears children, and passes her life in great happiness
and harmony.

In this manner a week passed away, they tasted.
mutually delicious draughts of love. After some
longer time the hope of bearing pleasant fruit
was experienced by that heart-charming cypress.
Her body's beauty languished, and the expression
of her countenance changed. Her ruddy com-
plexion became of a saffron hue. After nine
months she gave birth to a beautiful fairy, at
the sight of whose face all were delighted. On
the 21st day of November in the year 1840 " Mary
Louisa " was born, * and happy and auspicious
fortune smiled upon the mother. Some time passed

---

* On 21st November 1840 a daughter, Adelaide Mary
Louisa, was born, who on the 25th January 1858 was married
to Frederic William, Prince of Prussia.

after this event in rejoicing and merriment, night and day being spent in ease and comfort and good health. When again a happy time arrived in 1841 the narcissus again became affected, * the heart-charming rose put on beauty of another hue, the garden of the body bloomed afresh, and again the royal branch was yielding precious fruit. In the fulness of time it ripened and was ready ; and separating from the branch it took its place in the world. On the auspicious 9th of November a royal son was born, and prince Edward was the name given him. All know him by the title of Prince of Wales. In his lusty frame and bright forehead were seen true indications of royalty, in his face and chest, and hands and feet, he seemed a second Albert; while his noble

---

* Let it be understood that by the term 'narcissus' allusion is made here to Victoria's eyes ; for whether a woman is preg-nant or not is discovered by physicians from the appearance of her eyes, and from several other indications. On the 9th November 1841 the first son, the well known Albert Edward, Prince of Wales, was born. This eminent Prince is at present looked upon as the rightful heir of the English throne. It is said that he has been well educated in every branch of knowledge, by his late father and other teachers.

8 \

mien and appearance and deportment brought
to mind King William the Fourth. Every day
he gained the strength of a month, which occasioned great comfort to the heart of his mother.
All the people of England were glad, and there
was great excitement among his relations and
friends. Albert remembered God in his heart;
he bowed his head to the ground, and said, " O
hearer of the prayers of the faithful, Thou Lord of
wisdom, ocean of mercy, Thou only art in both
worlds stronger than all; by Thee only are all
virtues established; Thou hast conferred upon me
a blessing indeed, Thou hast blessed me by the
birth of a son; Thou hast made a bright lamp to
burn in the world, the English kingdom Thou
hast established, my humble name Thou hast exalted, in Thy mercy Thou hast fulfilled the desire
of my heart; in the garden of delight a fragrant
bud has expanded, Thou hast caused the hopeful
plant to bring forth fruit. Thanks that the moon
of the desire of the heart shines out from the
tower of hope; thanks that by this best
riches of the world my fortune has become
greatly beyond computation. I render Thee

innumerable thanks for these Thy favours, but any return for them it is never possible to make : though each hair of this body became a tongue and poured forth thanksgivings every moment to the judgment day, yet not a particle of this favour would be repaid, for by favours of this sort alone can the world continue to be inhabited."

Always give thanks, O brother, for nothing of thine will continue unless thou do give thanks. Thanksgiving alone makes gifts blessings, and without thanksgiving all gifts become curses. The tree of prosperity remains fruitful through thanks, without thanks it is consumed to ashes.

By this event England became glad, in every house there was eating, drinking, and dancing ; feast upon feast was celebrated in every town, and words of congratulation passed between all, whether high or low. The Prince was brought up with every care ; and graces worthy of royalty appeared in him. Some time afterwards, this royal tree again becoming fruitful, bore a beautiful daughter,* and continued after this to bear in due season, so that producing sons and daughters it caused the royal family to increase exceedingly. The favour of God came down without measure; England became as it were a peaceful rose garden. The spring of peace and tranquillity bloomed there, the sword of war and vengeance was sheathed. Through peace the world became fragrant as a rose, oppression fled away, and truth and faith took up their abode in it; streams of justice flowed upon all sides; the fire of tyranny and imposition was extinguished, and the Queen occupied her throne in the enjoyment of the utmost happiness and

---

* That is to say, after the birth of the Prince of Wales another daughter, by the name of Alice Mary, was born on the 25th April 1843 ; and after her, on the 6th August 1844 another son, named Alfred Ernest ; on the 25th May 1846 a third daughter, Helena Augusta ; on the 18th March 1848 a fourth daughter, Louisa Caroline ; and on the 1st May 1850 Arthur William Patrick, a third son ; on the 7th April 1853 a fourth son, Leopold George Duncan ; and after him, on the 14th April 1857 a fifth daughter, Beatrice Mary. Thus four sons and five daughters were born to the most gracious, fortunate, and exalted Queen Victoria, and by the grace of God these are all still living, and are engaged in various ways in the active duties of life.

honour. Albert and Victoria lived happily, no other pair in the world could enjoy such happiness. No other have existed so loving and beloved as that a report of their faults has not gone abroad among the people, no other have lived in this frail world in perfect purity and love such as theirs.

CHAPTER V.

———∘∘⦂❀⦂∘∘———

Prince Albert and Victoria live together a long time perform-
ing their duties of life in a most exemplary manner,
and Albert takes the lead with great zeal in good works
of every kind, &c.

Know, O reading brother, that this exalted royal
pair lived together 20 years subsequently to 1840
in the enjoyment of every kind of happiness and
dignity; ruling the English nation, which possessed supremacy over all the nations of the
earth. What shall I say of the fortunes of the
Queen! The rolling heaven was as it were, under
her control, her will was like a chogan,* and
the whole world like a ball revolved around her.
Great and mighty kings became subject to her.
She cut off the heads of the rebellious, and desolate
became the country of the cruel Pindárís. All
the capital cities of ancient kings bowed humbly
before her. Proud China was brought low as if the

---

* See a former note on this word.

days of the warlike Janges Khan had returned; *
the heroic Punjabees were completely subdued, as
if it were again the days of Alexander. Sind
and Afganistan were humbled, as if Zalezar the
son of Nariman had come to life again; terror
was struck into the hearts of Pegu and Java.
The lofty pomp of Burmah passed away, and
the pride of Mahomedan Persia was as much
abased as if the day of Ardasheer Babegan had
revived. And besides these the whole of Hin-
doostan was brought under her dominion; the
power of the princes of all classes was broken.

The Prince and the Queen enjoyed to the
full the riches and precious things of this world;
the wealth of their fame in the earth spread
honour and virtue among every race, obtained

---

* Janges Khan was the chief of the country of Tartary.
About the year 1200 he conquered China, and reigned there,
and under his government and that of his successors the
Mahomedan religion spread in that country. This chief was
at first engaged in the humble profession of a blacksmith,
but being naturally very intelligent and brave he became in
short time a mighty emperor. The native historians of China
state that in the great battles of this hard-hearted chief a mil-
lion men were killed in sixteen days, and this slaughter was
followed by a pestilence which destroyed 900,000 more.

the respect of their own people and of foreigners, conferred favours and obligations upon the needy, and gained the love of their friends and companions. Albert was affable to all, and applied his wisdom to every subject. He possessed such a store of learning that learned men applied to him for advice continually.

All the ministers and accomplished statesmen of the kingdom considered it an honour to ask his opinion; by the bright piercing rays of his judgment he illuminated the beclouded hearts of hundreds. There was no good Society in London without his patronage, and so great was the confidence which England reposed in him that Parliament made a special law that if (it being the will of God for such a calamity to happen) the virtuous Victoria should die without an heir, Prince Albert should be king, that all England should bow to his authority, that due respect according to the law should be paid to him, and all his lawful commands be carried out. By the passing of such a law the influence of Albert was greatly increased in every assembly.

The story of his virtues spread in the whole world, and Germany rejoiced with exceeding joy. All the poor labourers of England found patronage, encouragement, and sustenance from him. He patronised all kinds of industry, for all claimed his support on one pretext or another. He paid great attention to education, and took the lead in advancing the arts. He looked with favour on all places of learning, and perfected himself in the knowledge of every science. He had a fervent love for the indigent, and had no prejudice against receiving the poor; loving industry he was always industrious. He set on foot a novel scheme which revived the arts of the whole world, and from which the industrious derived abundance of profit. In the year 1851, he accomplished a work at once great and good. He toiled intensely with body, soul, and intellect; and established a great museum, expended upon it much patience and thought, and drew the attention of the whole world to it. He gave encouragement to every manufacture, and imparted as it were new life to the world. Day and night he made great personal exertions in the cause,

9 A

and by his sagacious measures he obtained money
for it from the imperial treasury. He assisted
it, moreover, from his own resources. He was
ready in hand and liberal in heart, he collected together the manufactures of the whole world, and
caused others to admire and patronise whatever
was excellent. He set a value on every thing
according to its workmanship, and distributed
money and goods as prizes, giving also medals
to the most skilful artists. In fine he sought
the welfare of the poor of all countries, and caused
the rich to purchase the products of the industry
of the poor; and he was successful in carrying
out the whole of his design.

All these things becoming known to the sovereigns of the world, the light of Albert's fame
spread every where. He met with similar success
in every other undertaking, and obtained the love
of high and low. A meeting of nobles and people from every quarter assembled together, and
expressed their thorough appreciation of Albert's
deeds. In every possible way they showed him
honour, and all praised his wisdom. Albert
then made this reply :—

" Before all things I thank the Lord that so great and extensive a work has been carried out in so successful a manner, that great and learned men like you have continued throughout it in harmony and unanimity. It indeed becomes us to acknowledge, with all our hearts, our obligations to that God, by whose grace and mercy and compassion our efforts have been crowned with success. Our entire aim has been fulfilled, the mercy of the Lord has been with us to the end. But let us also beseech Him that this our good and benevolent undertaking may tend to the profit of the whole world, and that the labourers of all nations may become more and more skilful, may be able to discriminate between excellences and defects in all things, and that in design and execution they may greatly improve; that a spirit of true emulation may arise in their minds, that they may vie with each other in skill, fight the battles of the arts with the force of their intellects, and win fame and wealth in the fields of knowledge. Wise men heartily approve of works of this kind, which produce concord be-

tween each other's countries, which enable
one nation to become intimately acquainted
with another, and promote friendship and mutual
esteem between them; bring distant countries
into close relationship, and breathe unity of
sentiment between different tribes and races.
This event must be considered good; the rays of
its goodness will diffuse themselves throughout
all time, the darkness of folly will be removed,
and the people of the world will obtain profit
and joy."

CHAPTER VI.

———◦◦◦◦———

Prince Albert becomes president and patron of several public bodies, and takes the Queen to his native country.

IN this way he was always engaged giving his valuable aid to every good work. He took a leading part in many public meetings, and always made effective speeches. His voice was soft and musical, his style elegant and attractive, every sentence was full of eloquence, in which shone forth the light of even-handed justice. Some felt his frank speaking to be distasteful,* but the wise heartily approved of it. Were we to give

---

* "The late Prince Albert was connected with every useful public body in England, becoming their patron; was constantly engaged in beneficent works, and made very powerful speeches. Besides Wellington College, and the Horticultural Society, many other institutions were greatly improved and rendered more stable under his presidentship. The speeches he made were collected and published by the Society of Arts, at the suggestion of Lord Ashburton, in the year 1857, and are well worthy of perusal. His speech was so fair and im-

an account of his speeches it would be tediously long. Were we to write the details of his actions and conduct, there would be need of another volume; therefore having given the above few particulars of them, we pass on. *If by the grace of God our life lasts, our heart's desire be granted us, and our health of body and mind preserved,*

---

partial that, more than once it drew upon him the wrath and disapprobation of several great men of England, as well as of the bishops and clergy of the Roman Catholic church. The great and honourable position of Chancellor of the University of Cambridge had been held by the Duke of Cumberland, but he died in 1847, and it was the wish of all the clergy and the ministers of religion of high rank that Earl Powis, a renowned, learned and influential nobleman, should be appointed in his room, and they lost no opportunity of using their influence to carry out their purpose; but the people of England had so high an opinion of Prince Albert's learning, wisdom and suavity of manners, that when a large public meeting was called and votes were taken as to the appointment to the Chancellorship abovementioned, Earl Powis obtained 837 and Prince Albert 953, and on the 6th July when the ceremony of his induction into the office took place, there was a great gathering, Her most excellent Majesty Victoria, and the kings and princes of several foreign countries, as well as all the great ministers of state being present. By this Albert was greatly delighted, and he continued to the last hour of his life to introduce, after considerable pains, and to carry out by the strength of his intellect and wisdom, many improvements and reforms in matters relating to that University."

*if particulars worthy of the subject be obtained,
if the Government, filled with justice, continue
gracious, we will again give our attention to this
subject.*

In 1843 a desire came into the heart of
Albert to visit his lovely native country,
whereupon he spoke these words to the Queen;
" O virtuous, heart-charming lady, the crown of
all the men and women of this world, I have a
wish that we should all go to Germany, and see
again the sights of bygone days: we shall find
companions and friends and loving ones, and
shall be delighted with the scenery of the country. How much longer time shall we pass in a
single place. There is no trusting this short
life, nothing lasts here for ever, there is no pleasure in the world like that derived from an
excursion; there is no love like the love of
one's own country. Therefore be then quickly
ready, and be willing with body and soul to
travel." When the Queen heard these words she
heartily complied with his wishes. She made
preparations suitable to her royal position, and
wrote and did all that was necessary.

Having fixed upon an auspicious day they commenced their journey, and were borne along by a horse of fire. As the arrow flies from the bow, or as the torrent rushes in the tempest, so went forth that steed of fire puffing forth steam from within him; step by step he cleaved the surface of the waves, made the sea foam with passion, and the plain of the ocean to quake beneath his rapid strides. He was furious as a leopard, destroying the inhabitants of the deep; he broke through the ranks of hundreds of whales, the waters of the sea stood aside doing obeisance to him. Tossing his head, he pressed forward incessantly night and day; and reaching his destination safely and securely, arrived at the appointed place, and finished with joy the passage of the sea.

The royal pair landed on the shore: crowds of people gathered to see them, all gave them due honour; and, taking up their abode in the royal palace, they remained for some days in the City of Gotha. Albert felt the ground of his native country dear to him; they visited every village and field, and wood: with every scene the Queen was delighted. When they saw the land of Rosina, the pleasant grief of past remembrance came to the heart of Albert! A stream of tears flowed from his eyes, when he remembered the scenes of his childhood. Seeing the place of his birth, the ground he had played in, the trees he had climbed, the fountains he had bathed in, the rose gardens of his delight,* the plains, the woods, the lengthy roads, the pure rivers, the clear brooks and the lofty mountains; he wept with sobs and sighs. Then collecting himself he spoke thus :—

SONG.

Thousand thanks that I have seen to-day,
My fatherland, O beloved.
The dry narcissuses have found the bloom of spring again.
The message of hope has come to this broken heart again.
The withered rosary of this body has,
As it were, become fresh again.
Wherever my beloved one will place her blessed footsteps,
There, in exceeding fragrance, will spring up roses and tulips.
O my country! I forgot thee not, at length I came back to thee.

---

* It is said that Prince Albert possessed great proficiency and skill in gymnastic exercises, as well as in the use of arms and in hunting. Once or twice he suffered from sickness in consequence of excessive fatigue from hunting.

10 A

The bird of my heart is caught in thy love
As the prey of the hunter.
When my eyes fell upon thy Joseph-like face,
In my soul, as in Zuleika, arose the intoxication of love.
O happy minded brother, consider base the soul of him
In whose heart dwelleth not the love of his native country.

The Prince bestowed the love of his heart upon his country, and showed the Queen all its varied sights, with which, as they passed in their journey over the mountains, she felt truly delighted. When they reached their final resting place, all people, high and low, came forth to meet them. Afterwards Victoria and Albert interchanged visits with their relations and friends, bestowed on the poor alms and gifts, and engaged themselves in deeds of charity and benevolence. Then both these renowned ones returned, and arrived in England in safety, where, seeing their faces, their subjects felt delighted.

CHAPTER VII.

Albert gives his eldest son necessary education, and imparts
to him counsels and advice worthy of his royal station.

In this manner several years passed, and Albert lived with Victoria in perfect happiness, and showed deference to the will of his beloved one. His advice made the old man youthful. With justice he tied the hands of wickedness, with understanding he made broad the path of religion, with the good he talked ably; the vicious trembled from fear of him; the poor worshipped the dust of his feet. He kept his heart pure with thoughts of God. He stood aloof from affairs of state, he imparted to his children the light of knowledge, cautioned them on every subject, led them to shun what was bad, and to embrace what was good. He bestowed gifts with a father's love, and showed favour to them in every thing. One day he called his eldest son, the sight of whose face raised his hopes, and lifting up his eyes to the lofty heavens, he said: *O beneficent Giver, Thy favours to me are innumerable, my heart is overwhelmed with Thy fear, continue to me Thy wonted aid, and preserve my honour and reputation; be Thou the Guide of this my son, fortify him with every virtue.*

HYMN.

O hearer of prayer, hear my petition!
I seek Thy will alone.
      (O hearer of prayer.)

Many a day and night have I wandered in the world,
But never found I one who wanted not, save Thee.
      (O hearer of prayer.)

Remaining a companion with him here, keep in good paths
This only hope of my heart, my son.
      (O hearer of prayer.)

In things temporal and spiritual give him Thy aid.
Considering him by nature poor, be gracious unto him.
      (O hearer of prayer.)

Lord of all power! remove dangers from him,
Putting away pain of body, create in him happiness of
  mind.
      (O hearer of prayer.)

Then he said to his son, O good son, now that thy years have become ripe, thy mother has great hopes of thee, all England places dependence upon thee. The coming time will try thee, and test whether thou art amber or straw, whether thou art a pearl having externally a royal shell, or whether thou art merely an outside glitter, being within false and base. Therefore my son, open thine eyes and ears ; seeing and hearing, understand this world of cares. Reading, bring to thy memory past events ; learn from history the stories of thy ancestors, and see how the people of the world have judged them after their death ; how they have sung their virtues, and how their vices; and learn therefrom the Providence of God, what is the end of virtue or vice, how one brings a good name and the other disgrace. Besides this it is my duty also to impart to thee a knowledge of the world in every thing. Having educated and trained thee, I have made thee ready ; like a parrot thy mouth speaks, but I do not see yet any sign that thy heart is enlightened with wisdom. Thy age is yet very tender ; thy understanding seems yet very deficient ; therefore hear thou these my words : arouse from sloth thy body and spirit, and know that in the field of this world good and evil of every kind are sown, but the plant which grows high in virtue becomes a power in the community; it obtains throne and crown and might, gives the protection of its shade to others; with the water of justice quenches the fire of the oppressor, and nourishes plants pleasing to the hearts of all, from which can be culled most precious fruits, making the world delightful; it establishes the root of virtue upon earth, and obtains the love of God and man. But in the man who aspires after such a position as this, every virtuous quality is required, his mind must be stored with the sweet words of counsel and warning. Attend thou then to the learning of bygone scholars; the wise man who acts in accordance with this does not meet in the world with curses and losses; it is as it were a treasury of happiness for this life, which beneficent philosophers give without charge. Those who do not store their minds with this treasure never obtain, in this world, virtue or friendship. I give thee this advice for thy future guidance, which the wise and the ignorant alike may understand.

Words of advice spoken by Albert to his eldest son,
the Prince of Wales.

(About Industry and painstaking.)

O my son, always be industrious, in good
labours thou wilt find no loss; only those
who labour are truly fortunate. The labour of
the body gives enjoyment to the soul. As a
diamond does not come forth unless the stone
is broken, so none can get name or honour
without toil. As a pen is useless for writing
except it be pointed, so without industry none
will obtain any profit in the world. On him
who keeps his hands in constant use, honour
and wealth are showered, but wealth has no
connexion with idleness, the mouth of an idle
man is shut. Wealth does not depend on fate,
wealth is only a firm companion of industry.
The various forms of industry and toil in this
world are the wards of the key of honour and
wealth; he from whose body drops the sweat
of toil, gets from the dry dust abundance of
wealth and honour; therefore, O son, never remain unemployed; and having toiled, acknowledge thy obligation to the Lord.

(About preserving a contented mind.)

There is nothing better than contentment: let thy heart be satisfied even upon a dry crust. He whose mind's eye is satisfied with the things on the surface of the tray of this world, will be exalted in the end; in the sea of giving and receiving he will remain full of brightness, as a pearl, which exists without water and air. Know the man who is contented to be a tree bringing forth flowers and fruits in all the four seasons. A heart with empty hands should be filled with contentment, for a hollow flute played by a Lokman * subdues a warrior. A contented man is not harassed with difficulties, as the lustre of a pearl is not lost in a famine. Patience opens the gates of fortune, impatience brings upon the head the stones of grief; by patience a stone is converted into a millstone, which by grinding prepares food for the contented man. The just Lord is so merciful that he supplies all according to their necessities, he gives as many grains

---

* A famous musician.

to each ear of corn as there are husky cells
to receive them. The virtue of contentment
is not general among the people of the world.
Mankind from the beginning have a desire to
obtain more and more. When the sucking child
has sucked one breast it stretches its hand
to the other. He who contentedly drinks the
blood of his heart, will, like a ruby, possess
value and greatness. A contented man does
not possess avaricious desires. Homa is not
caught in a net as a prey, through looking
at grain. Contentment shuts the lips against
slanderous questions. The brave man who
reposes upon the strength of the Lord, has
his desires accomplished in both the worlds.
As Solomon obtained victories by putting on
a ring,* so he who will rivet the attention of body and mind upon contentment
will obtain a dignified position, spiritually and

---

* It is said of king Solomon that he had a wonderful ring,
which he put on his finger whenever he wanted to get a
victory, and having done so he obtained the victory. In
the above passage the allusion is to show that the man who
possesses contentment will accomplish all things, and obtain
greatness

temporally. Consider the contented man a true alchymist, for by patience he turns the dry dust into gold. As Homa would not eat out of the mouth of a dog, so a contented man would not desire a boon from an avaricious one. Patience gives victory over difficulties, patience gives hope to the hopeless; by patience imperishable treasures are obtained, by patience stone is turned into diamonds, by patience innumerable dangers are avoided : all locks can be opened with the key of patience.

(About truth or veracity.)

God is a lover of straightforward conduct. By crooked courses man is ruined, through growing crookedly thorns come on the body of the rose tree, through growing straight the sugarcane is filled with sweetness. No man falls into distress by straightforward conduct, but by it remains ever happy; his mind and body bloom in every season, even calamity has no effect upon him. The face of him who raises high the banner of truth remains lustrous as the sun. There is such protection under the guidance of truth that even a man blind in body and mind may find the proper path; from even the lowest depths of the sea he may obtain deliverance and may ride upon the highest of the heavens. If in the bent bow of a man's mouth there is the pointed arrow of a fitting tongue, all the virtuous will give him honour, and having placed him above their heads will devote their lives to him.

(On Lying.)

O virtuous son, never speak thou an untruth. Bankers throw away all false coins. Know that the filth of sinful works exists in the heart of him whose tongue is defiled with lying, and the lamp of his soul is never bright. The flame of a crooked lamp soon goes out, so by untruthfulness all honour is cast to the winds.

(On concealing the faults of others.)

That robe gives grace to a man which covers without proclaiming the defects of the garments underneath. Keep thine eye shut as regards the faults of other men, for by so doing thy own virtue will be preserved. The naked man, who does not cover his own body, does not see any reasonableness in the complaints of other people. Shame and disgrace fall upon a backbiter; a writing reed, which is double-tongued, is always kept cut. Never divulge the secrets of others, even though thou wert hundred-tongued; as the eye, the pupil of which remains silent, for in divulging the secrets of others there is great crime. As the touchstone, after declaring metal to be base gold, becomes black, so the man who exposes another's fault, becomes himself ignominious. Learn this lesson from the pupil of the eye, seeing bad or good, say nothing at all. Consider him truly pious who by his virtues only makes himself a residence in the hearts of mankind. By spitting upon the heavens thou thyself will be spit upon; by slandering good people thou thyself wilt be abased. To make a useless noise by being a picker of faults is altogether dishonourable to a man; to bark behind one is the work of worthless dogs, the wise are not defamed by such conduct. There is true honour in seeing one's own faults, and much goodness in not seeing the faults of others.

(On the beauty of humility.)

Before the honourable show thou humility; wherever there is an arch, truly thou must bend. Humility will preserve thy life from oppression. No injury is done to cotton by a sword, but when soft water becomes a hard pearl it is troubled day and night with the fear of being pierced through. There is no better devotion than profound submission; haughtiness has, as it were, no life in this world. Truly wise men are modest in their speech, as the mouths of bottles full of wine are shut. If thou wishest the old and the young should be thy friends, keep not thy body straight as an arrow, but keep thyself bent as a fruitful bough bestowing loads of favours upon the needy. Nature has given thee a teethy millstone, therefore ruminate and make thy speech tender. A weak swimmer makes a sign by lifting up his hand, so know him to be a wise man who acknowledges his own weakness. As soft milk melts hard sugar, so sweet words dissolve anger. If thou remain flexible as the string of a rosary, thou wilt conquer difficulties moment after moment. Humility finds a home in the hearts of people, as a fine thread enters the eye of a needle; as a thread becomes a vein in the body of a pearl, so a wise man cherishes humility. Worshipping people lay their heads upon the ground, but do thou place that low which is inside the head. The whole of God's law may be on thy lips, but if the devil be in thy heart how will the evil be remedied? Never practise in any way self-exaltation, for the exalter of self never attains to eminence. Loving not thyself obtains the love of others; not receiving any injury, do good to others. Where there is humility there is an indication of good origin, even as by its flexibility a sword is known to be of fine temper. When through humility this earth becomes dust, the heavens paint their eyes as with collyrium. He whose outward height is little will have a correspondingly small share of grief and fear. When the fury of the wind falls upon trees the growing reed remains happy and tranquil. A man of low origin may be as high as the sun, but the taint of meanness will never go from his heart.

If the heavens were not bent with humility, they would not be in every place above this world. When a dry grain becomes as dust, growing and blooming, it supports the living creatures of the earth. By humility difficult works become easy. A painter draws a picture of a mountain with a hair. Nature has given such honour to the soft dew that the sun lifts it on high with the wire of its ray. If thou wishest to receive much honour in weighing thyself with others, make thyself less.

(On the advantages of travelling.)

The wise are much benefited by travels. As a polisher of metals cleans off rust, so by travelling a man becomes polished and refined; the taint of an evil destiny is removed by travelling. By travelling the qualities of the good and bad are brought to light: as long as an arrow remains concealed in the quiver, so long it does not appear to others whether it is exactly straight or crooked, but when having come forth from its recess, and rested on the bow, it goes towards a spot aimed at, its excellence or defect is perceived. Had Joseph not left his own country how would Zuleika have been enamoured of him ? and how would he have attained a royal position upon earth ? On those who are fond of remaining in their own country, various sorts of evils fall. As long as a rose remains attached to its branch it suffers annoyance from the piercing thorn. A traveller is always entertained with amusements, and by experience he attains to perfection. By travelling, sympathy for man is acquired ; to the enterprising man his own country is a prisoner's cell. As long as a gem is shut up in its stone, nobody knows its worth or value, so he who abides only in his own country will never obtain praise or worldly greatness. As long as a cornelian remains in the country of Yemen its full value or price is not discovered. Were growing trees to take a journey, the saw would not cut their body or head. Without travelling intelligence is not made manifest, just as words are only formed when the breath issues forth. When a disagreeable man leaves his own country and goes elsewhere, he becomes beloved. Learned men never rest in their own country. Ripe fruits abandon the branch and the tree.

(On purity of heart.)

There is nothing better than a pure heart. He who fights against a pure heart will in the end repent; he who dashes against a dagger will assuredly be pierced. As there is no darkness in the eye of the sun, so no filth of revenge dwells in a pure heart. As the rays of the sun are the dress of the morning, so in the heart of a pure man there dwells the brightness of light. As the heart of a mirror cannot be scratched with the finger nail, so it is utterly useless to fight against a simple-hearted man. As quick-silver does not stand still on a plate of glass, so does not revenge rest in a pure bosom. A pure heart does not require worldly armour : one pure heart is proof against a hundred warriors. A true heart is not injured by slander, as smoke does not remain in a bright lamp. Without a pure heart strength of body is vain ; with a rusty sword slaughter cannot be effected. A pure hearted man sees all his works ; through purity only the eyes see all things from a distance. As there is no flood of rains in the sea, so there

12 A

is no revenge in the pure heart of a friend against a friend. A pure heart becomes a mirror for the face of a friend. A pure-hearted man is a friend to every one, as a mirror gladdens all people alike by reflecting their faces. Be on thy guard against deceiving a pure heart; by breathing upon a mirror thou wilt see darkness.

(On the cunning and craftiness of enemies.)

Never trust in the soft speech of an enemy, for the bent bow is ready for its prey. As death does not show forbearance to an old man, so the receiving of reverence does not save one's life from an enemy. He who reposes trust in the soft speech of an enemy is considered in the world perfectly senseless. The water of the flood, which falls beneath the feet, razes buildings to the ground in a moment; the axe which kisses the feet of the tree, in the end cuts off its body, its head, and its branches. When the haughty yields before thy strength, never repose confidence in him, for a gentle fire will still do fire's work; where from inadvertence it falls it will burn every thing. A soft exterior may be hard within; in soft cotton there are the knots of its hard seeds. As a hunter, stooping, seeks for prey, so a deceiver, bending, performs obeisance. Be ever on thy guard against the union of thy enemies: ants united can wreak vengeance upon a tiger. If a wicked enemy speak soft words, then know thou the contrary, that he is plotting: know that in a soft morsel there may be a hard bone, which will hurt the throat suddenly. Never be incautious after the defeat of an enemy; beneath the grass there is often a pit for destruction.

(On liberality and the liberal man.)

True liberality is true righteousness; in true liberality there is infinite virtue. That is liberality which does not expect any return, in interested liberality there is sin. He who expends gold to make his own name, will be unapproved in the courts of the Lord. As in one sprinkling the cloud fills the shell, so do truly liberal men give relief to the needy. By favours a wicked man finds calmness; a satisfied stomach is a chain to the temper of a tiger. The hand of the liberal man who expends his wealth on good objects, shall, like the sea, never be emptied. If the Lord has bestowed on thee the blessing of wealth, be not negligent in finding out the condition of thy friends. Never murmur while showing liberality, and do not sigh if thanks are withheld. Abandonment of wealth and property is not liberality : by giving to the needy thou wilt attain to heaven. If thou hast wealth, show kindness to the needy: wealth, hoarded in a cell, will never become a mine. If thou improve the condition of the poor by thy wealth, thou wilt be delighted with happiness in the future world ; the rich man who does not sympathise with the distresses of the poor, imperceptibly throws his wealth into air ; but the wealthy man who lends a helping hand to the afflicted, remains in the world firm and immoveable. Wealth is a lantern, but liberality is a lamp around which is the greatest true happiness. Generally the works of the people continue shut up like a bud : as the breath of spring, do thou open them. Keep the mouth of thy purse open like a rose, do not keep gold shut up like a bud. He is good who becomes a patron of the good, he is truly heroic who lifts up the fallen. If thou wouldst possess true manliness be thou generous. He is truly a man who is lord over the lust of self. On the forehead of him who lifts up his foot and kicks the fallen, clings the brand of unmanliness. If thou canst with thy own nails loosen the knot of any one, do not wait for the help of others. If thou dost not wish to have the help of a stick in thy old age, in thy youth hold the hand of the fallen. Charity is a coverer of every fault, parsimony is the destroyer of wisdom and skill. As the clouds sprinkle precious water without charge, and do not make any distinction between a bamboo and a sugarcane, so do liberal men go on giving good gifts, considering the good and bad alike. Truly charity is precious in the world, nevertheless in it these two points are above all: First, to give before asking; and secondly, to impose no obligation upon the receiver. As the beam of a balance lifts up the scales hanging low, so he who possesses naturally a large heart lifts up the fallen ones, and makes them stand erect. As the rain falls upon the rose and thorn alike, so do thou look with an equal eye upon all. As after scattering pearls the rain does not wait for a return; so, truly liberal men see greatness only in giving. Every one eats bread in the world according to his destiny, the generous Lord is the author of all good things; if thou hast understanding, be thou the means of distributing them. Be thou here prominent as the sun, that, after thou art set, the world may be black with mourning. By conferring favours, sleeping wealth becomes awake, as the inactive brain becomes quickened by a sneeze. As, for the good of others, the lamp rides the whole night in fire and water, so do thou spend thy body and mind, day and night, to be an alleviator of the griefs of others. As the rose holds gold in its open hand, so hold thou thy head in the palm of thy hand, for the sake of thy friend. He who, without seeking his own profit, undertakes the support of a blind man, procures the falling of the hand of blessing upon all his works. Man's true greatness consists in giving, and God's full blessing is bestowed upon this service.

(On the evils of avarice.)

The hope of an avaricious man clings to gold, the bounties of the world can never quench his thirst. As a fish with many scales has numerous bones, so is there a great weight of anxiety on the heart of a wealthy man. As it is a well known habit of some foppish men to take more care of their hats than of their heads, so wealth is dearer to misers than their own souls. They neglect their souls to preserve their gold. Kahrun* in his avarice, went into the depths of the sea to obtain wealth from the belly of a fish. If any one wishes to live happily he must banish avarice from his heart altogether. An avaricious man cannot be brave hearted. The slave of avarice requires no chains : honey even is the means of the death of flies. As the belly of the hungry cannot be filled without eating, so an avaricious man can never be satisfied without riches.

* A notorious miser of the East.

(On the evil of niggardliness.)

A miser with infinite care weaves a net for gold, and makes the bird of his soul captive in avarice. There is a saying all over the earth against misers, " With the blood of misers hands would not be reddened." The condition of nothing is so bad as that of the hoarded wealth of the miser. The gold of a miser lifts up its voice in complaint and murmuring, and casts ashes on its body for grief every moment. As labourers lift up the bags of money, so misers labour after gold, fruitlessly. It is a peculiarity natural to misers to give abuse to the needy when they ask any thing of them. A miser becomes such an enemy to the world that nobody laments his death. A painted moon does not give light, so liberality is naturally far away from a miser. As when filth is collected in a cesspool wise and sensible men keep away from it, so when a mean man becomes filled with money, keep thyself aloof from his company. A dog cannot rival Homa, though a dog is also fond of bones. Man's heart is the mirror of all secrets; it is a pity that with a seeing eye a man becomes blind. As the meshes of a net cannot be filled with dry dust, so a niggardly man cannot be satisfied by a profusion of bounties.

(On the Excellence of Justice and Equity.)

Justice and equity are required in a king, that all his subjects may be gladdened by their beauty. One hour's justice is thought better than a hundred years of life to an emperor. By the influence of justice a country prospers, by justice only the throne of the sovereign is established, by justice only the name of a king endures. He who dispenses a moment's justice in this world makes his eternal happiness secure in the next.

(On the evil of Tyranny.)

Never remain ignorant of thy own affairs; do not live senselessly in the world. If under false pretences thou oppress others, wise men will abhor thee. An act of oppression brings sorrow

13 A

of mind. Do not think an evil thought of this kind, that there is no voice in a broken-hearted being, for its voice will be lifted up in the day of judgment, and in the next world it will make thee completely miserable. When a king withdraws his hands from oppression, his life is prolonged by the blessings of the people. As a chain itself endures perpetual bondage, so an annoyer of the afflicted will never see happiness. Do not expect any thing but oppression from an oppressor; in burning mountains there is essentially a fiery nature. A poisonous tree does not bear sweet fruits, every thing exists according to its peculiar kind. As if a sword breaks, it turns into a dagger, so a tyrannous man will always be a cruel tyrant. As the walking of a scorpion brings destruction upon itself, so the wickedness of the wicked brings about their own ruin. An oppressor can never become happy by his evil deeds, any more than a bee can ever get to taste a drop of its own honey. As the house of the bee is digged out and becomes a lamp, so when the house and possession of an oppressor are destroyed, people put up bright lamps there, and pronounce upon him curses and imprecations. Do not cast the fire of oppression upon the fallen, for lightning striking the ground becomes destroyed. As the rapidity of a flood shortens it own existence, so upon the oppressor himself is the effect of his oppression.

(About Friends.)

As a weak eye obtains strength from spectacles, so he who keeps company with a pure hearted man would obtain sight even if he were blind. As is one's company, so are his thoughts; in the company of the tulip the dew becomes red; in the company of the good there is great virtue. By association with *Пота* bones become of value. Solitude makes a man truly intelligent, but it is by good company only that he becomes perfect. We may be bruised like grains with a millstone, but from a suitable hearted friend we should never separate. To the bad the company of the good is like armour, the arrows of the evil have no effect upon him. As the wick of the heart of a candle burns, so if friends burn together in their hearts and become of one opinion, the lamp of each one's fortune will be bright, and the darkness of misfortune be altogether removed. Do not abandon thy friends and live solitary, for solitude does not comport with any, save God. If thou desirest happiness, temporal and eternal, never turn thy face from a virtuous friend; when the hand removes the wire from *tumbura*, it loses its heart-attracting tunes; by the company of the good a good influence is exerted: a gem makes a brass ring precious. Upon the truly virtuous no effect is wrought by the wicked, as the salt sea does not affect the lustre of a pearl. The worthy are affected by the worthy, the fragrance of the rose does not descend into the branch.

(On the evil of bad company.)

The young man who sits with women will paint his own face with the colour of shame. Bad company brings distress upon a well disposed man, as a broken leg prevents the motion of the whole body. By companionship with a coward, the brave loses his courage; his honour, self-respect, and reputation, all depart. If a fire, a hundred years old, comes in contact with water, its heat will be destroyed in a moment; so the life-long virtue of a good man flies away in one hour by companionship with an evil one: the sun shining with boundless splendour is hidden by the intervention of a single cloud. If any one becomes thy friend on account of thy external circumstances, never place confidence in him, but consider such friendship like the reflection in a mirror, which will be faithful only just as long as it is seen. The sinful do not become holy by the company of the virtuous, as the effect of poison is not removed by sugar. As when fire and water come in contact a struggle arises instantly, so no union can last between two opposite-tempered men. Be upon thy guard with an evil man, continue towards him as a stranger, for thou wilt fall into a net if thou eat a grain of food with him. As when the bow is bent the arrow abandons its companion, and goes straight off through hundreds of yards of space, and as when one scale of a balance receives a slight weight it

forsakes its old companion; so the unfaithfulness
of a naturally bad companion, will lead him, on
a slight pretext, to give up thy friendship. In
the company of the rich thou wilt not see any
good, as in the company of the pearl the thread
remains unsteady. As in the cold season the
black night is lengthened, so in the company of
the afflicted afflictions increase. As the life of
the thread in the needle grows less, so in the
company of the narrow-minded a man loses his
feeling of compassion. As the bright morning
flies from the night, so fly thou from the hands
of the black-hearted.

———oo◦⟨◦⟩◦oo———

(On Riches; the rich man; and poverty.)

Verily in the garden of the world there are
people ever weeping from the pain of empty
hands; their blood boils in their hearts as roses
are boiled to make rosewater. They pass their
time in swallowing gulps of blood. The holy
mendicant dwelling in a temple burns with his
heart like a candle, in the hope of gold. Scholars, learned men, and devoted worshippers,

without gold, endure the affliction of poverty.
The gold of this world is so heart-charming that
the teachers of religion sell for it the pearl of
their pure conscience. By money a bad and
obscure name blooms, and the base performs
great works. He who keeps money ready in his
pocket, finds lustre like the light in the eyes of
the people. When a bottle is filled with wine
every body's arm is thrown around its neck, but
when it is empty nobody looks at it. Know thou
this to be the state of the poor; a brother does
not look at a brother without money; a maid
forgets her lover if he possesses not money; but
strangers with wealth become the relations of
rich men, for golden flowers find places on the
head. Poor men sell their goods cheap only,
by nature their fortune is of small value. The
greatest business of the world is gold; the richer
a man is, the wiser he is held to be. The thing
that makes men lion-like and brutish in disposition is poverty, poverty, yea poverty! As fishes
without scales are considered unclean, so when
wealth is lacking all vices come out. Money is
the cure for the poison of intense grief, money

soothes affliction and burning. The faults of the man who scatters money out of his pocket are hidden and screened. The dust of the hand holding gold is like *surma* applied to the eye, and the smoke of gold's lamp seems like light. On account of money only the poor suffer affliction; in the lamp of the poor there is always a flickering. The gold coloured wax in the ear teaches this one thing, that wherever there is gold, lend thy ears.

As long as thou hast gold in thy hand as the rose, hundreds of nightingales will continue devoted to thee. As empty bottles are thrown upon the shelf, and nobody casts more than a glance at them, so if a poor man sits in an exalted position the whole community regard him only with contempt. Baseness is never perceived in a rich man. Money alone is lord over all things. Debt abases the dignity of man, the debtor becomes light and the debt heavy.

————oo¦o¦oo————

(In imitation of an Ode of Kubeer.)

The whole play is of money,
Of all things money is the dearest. } Chorus.

By money is wife, by money sons,
By money kith and kin;
By money a companion keeps companionship,
By money come relations and friends.

      (The whole play, &c.)

By money religion, by money devotion,
By money goodness;
By money kings reign,
By money they make war.

      (The whole play, &c.)

All are enamoured with money only,
None with the heart.
By money one's nature is determined,
Without money his state is miserable.

      (The whole play, &c.)

If money for food and clothing is found,
The wife holds her hands respectfully.
If but one day food is not given,
She gives back impertinent answers.

      (The whole play, &c.)

Brothers, sisters, family connections,
All are brethren of money.
But when a companion dwells with the heart in affliction,
Consider his to be true faithfulness.

      (The whole play, &c.)

14 A

1.   O son, remember that evils arising in a kingdom are like unto evils engendered in the body of man.   As sundry evils of a kingdom are removed by threats, by chastisement, and by bestowing praise, so the body is cleansed of its evils by medicine, by surgery, or by plastering. In both cases it is a duty of paramount importance to choose means according to the nature of the evil, and it should be the aim of all true physicians and statesmen to remove first and thoroughly the source from which the evil arises, whatever that source may be, so that consequent evils may be averted.

2.   A person who is naturally jocular or one of a very hot temper must not be made head of an army.   From a chief of a joking disposition soldiers learn to show disrespect and disobedience, and instead of doing a thing at a critical time they begin to laugh and joke.   Also a man of very hot and cruel temper should not be appointed, for under such a chief the army is obliged to remain in fear of corporal punishment and fatigue; and consequently, being disaffected,

they consider it lawful to forget the right of the king to their gratitude and deference.

3. In a king jocularity and a tendency to laughter and jesting are not at all desirable; since through these he is not able to preserve his dignity and majesty before his servants and enemies; similarly haughtiness and melancholy are undesirable, because on account of these friends and lovers of justice shrink from making their requests and wants known to him, and injury is gradually done to him.

4. As physicians take fees as rightful earnings for preserving the health of mankind, or for improving the wasted condition of any sick man, so in return for protecting their country and for preventing quarrels, kings draw money from their subjects in the shape of taxes, fourths, rents, and other kinds of impositions; and this is just.

5. It is necessary to a king when he sends an ambassador to a foreign court that the ambassador be fluent, swift in speech, truth loving, mild tempered, and able to describe things dis-

tinctly; because an ambassador is, as it were, the tongue of a king, and through his sweet and suitable speech, the heart of the foreign king becomes well disposed to his master.

6. Engage frequently in secret consultation with persons who are wise and patient, sensible, quick minded, and experienced, with habits of forethought, and sterling honesty: unite them in subjects worthy to be kept as secrets, and in the things of thy heart unite them; because from doing this a good name and numberless advantages will accrue to thee.

7. Having bestowed honour upon persons of pure and holy minds, take care of them, and maintain regard for them; for in the time of war, as well as of peace, their prayers will be of great advantage to thee.

8. Maintain an intimate connection with the nobles and governors of every district of thy country, outwardly preserving their dignity, and reposing full confidence in them; but at the same time maintaining great vigilance and caution in reference to their works and behaviour.

9. Considering vuzeers, secretaries, and treasurers as the mirrors of the administration of thy state, look after them with great thoroughness, and without remissness; for by so doing the affairs of thy kingdom, the condition of thy subjects, and of thy army, and the accounts of thy revenue and expenditure will be known to and attended to by thee.

10. Always endeavour, by giving encouragement and help to physicians, learned and erudite men, to improve and increase the health of thy subjects and the education of their minds; and for this purpose keep the doors of thy treasury open.

11. Kings must keep entirely aloof from several hurtful things; as wine, gambling, chess, and things like them.

12. Kings, while conducting themselves courteously towards their powerful foes, must ever keep their weak enemies strongly pressed down; for if this is done, the powerful enemy will not suddenly venture to step beyond his own limits. With every enemy affection should be

outwardly maintained, according to his worth; for a powerful king is like an able gardener, his country being like a garden of fruits and flowers; the weak enemies who dwell round about that country being like the thorns and weeds of that garden; and when a powerful king keeps on terms of friendship with weak kings, beyond a certain limit, and does not watch over the cleanliness of his own garden, in a short time those thorns and weeds increase; that is, the weak enemies, having triumphed over the powerful king, defeat him. And as a good gardener goes round his garden, and removes dry grass and withered leaves, makes the dying plants live with water, that the garden may look bright and blooming, so does a wise king go about the country frequently, keep an eye on the prosperity of his dominions, remedy with all his heart the state of distressed subjects, and extinguishing oppression and tyranny, reign in justice.

13. There are three qualities necessary in the Commander-in-Chief of an Army; first, bravery; second, truth; third, experience in every

thing; and without these qualities a chief must be considered useless.

14.   By doing three things a king becomes negligent, does not do his work aright, and does not succeed in his wishes; first, the indulgence of lust, or of the company of women; second, indulgence of a desire for hoarding up wealth and property;   third, indulgence in wine and in eating intoxicating substances.

15.   It becomes thee not to commit great affairs to men of low birth and poor condition; for the burden of an elephant can never be lifted up by an ass.

16.   Revenue is like a fountain of water, and expenditure is like a running river: it becomes him who wishes to keep the river of expenditure running, to watch with great vigilance the waters issuing from the fountain.

17.   As a traveller, who thoughtlessly makes up such a bundle that he can get no man to carry, is prevented from fulfilling his design; so the man who goes on spending without looking at his income, will at the end be brought to poverty and starvation.

18.   A wise king seeks the prosperity of his subjects, for the prosperity of his subjects causes the prosperity of his treasury, and by the prosperity of his treasury the army remains contented and faithful; by the fidelity of the army the country obtains glory and peace; by the peace of the country, the duties of piety and religion are kept up; and when the duties of religion are kept up, God and the servants of God are pleased; and where God is pleased, there is abundance, and increase of all bounties, and when there is abundance of bounties, joy and gladness are universally diffused.

19.   It becomes a king not to interfere with any body's religion, and not to vex the poor; to watch over merchants and artizans, and by patronizing every industrious, skilful, and clever man, to advance his interests.

20.   It becomes a king not to rule otherwise than justly and truly. There is a proverb, " A flame of fire increases as the wind blows," but the flame of the fire of kingly oppression is extinguished by the wind of the sighs of the poor

and helpless; that is, the tyrannical career of the king soon comes to an end.

21. If thou wishest that God should love thee, it becomes thee not to be ignorant of that God.

22. Courtesy is necessary to a king, not haughtiness. Courtesy is a characteristic of truly pious men, but the attribute of the wicked is pride. Pride is a quality of fire, and Satan's essence is of fire; courtesy, that is affability, is a quality of dust, and man's origin is of dust.

23. It becomes a king not to make persons of noble descent and plunderers desperate, by keeping the former in poverty and the latter in a starved and wretched state; because when a gnat or a moth, by the intoxication of loneliness, becomes desperate, he clashes with a burning lamp; and sometimes it happens, that instead of burning himself he extinguishes the lamp.

24. As some of the lusts and passions of this body are always at war with lusts and passions of an opposite nature, and in order to keep down each other's ascendancy, they continue

the contest that the health of the body may be preserved ; so in order to preserve the dignity and greatness, the concord and peace, of a country, a king has to wage war, and to maintain struggles with other kings and other people.

25.   In this world a king is a divine shadow : and as the use of a shadow is to cool those who have suffered from the pain of heat, by taking them under its protection, so also must a king, being interested in the existing state of his subjects, servants and dependants, keep them full of happiness, under his own protection ; and as God in his goodness gives daily sustenance to his servants, so must a king, by making presents of gold and treasure to his officers and army, according to their service and worth, continually promote them to higher positions.

26.   As God is true and faithful, so also should a king be ; he should not tell the secrets of one officer to another, for if he be unfaithful, his officers will one day unite themselves, gird their loins to seek the destruction of the king, and keep all evil things hidden from him.

27.   As God is a dispenser of pardons and

a regarder of all persons alike, so should a king dispense strict justice to every one alike, be he lord or beggar, high or low, rich or poor.

28.   It becomes a king not to make a man of haughty and proud disposition a ruler, because under the rule of such a one disaffected and rebellious thoughts will spread among his subjects, the subjects forming an opinion of the whole government of a king from. what they see of the doings of one officer.   Whether therefore the king be bad or good, just or tyrannical, his subjects will judge him from the conduct of his officers.

29.   From the weak part of the body of man the canker of disease goes into another part, whence physicians deem it necessary to apply medicine to that part, so is it necessary that the place in the king's dominions whence a quarrel first arises be first put into perfect order.

30.   Merchants are the treasure of a king's dominions ; and know that the greater and better the care taken of this treasure, the greater the prosperity.   This prosperity is increased in two

ways; first, by good, clean, and safe roads; and secondly, through the king's strict justice and attention to complaints.

31. A king's country is like a beautiful woman, and the merchants of that country are, as it were, the precious jewels and ornaments of that woman; and the more these jewels and ornaments are, the more heart-charming and beautiful she looks.

32. Treasury and army both must be taken care of, as by the abundance of treasure an army may be increased, so if the army be strong gold may be obtained. Wise men say that gold is like honey; as long as busy bees continue to sit, and fly over the waxen comb with juice in their mouths, so long the comb continues to be filled with honey, but when the bees themselves forsake the cell and go away, if there were even hundreds of tons of honey, there would be no use for it; so if there be no strong and enterprising army, the treasure of the whole world would be of no use.

33. A king is a fountain of running water; and his ministers and officers are as it were the

rivers and brooks, which issue from that fountain. If the water of the fountain is sweet, the
water of those brooks and rivers must be sweet
too, but if that fountain is bitter, all these must
needs also be bitter ; that is, whatever be the
mien and disposition of a king, its influence will
be exercised over all his servants and dependants.

34. A king's heart must be like the clear
glass of a mirror, that charts and pictures of all
the events done in his country or in his court
may by him be easily seen ; that a black African
in the garb of a fairy, or a fairy in the garb of a
black African, may not succeed in any object
he may have in view ; and that whatever may be
the form and colour of any one's conduct it may
appear to him in its true light.

35. As nature has placed one tongue in the
mouth of a king, so his word should be one ; for
the tongue is as it were a messenger of the heart,
and the heart is a home of love or hatred ;
therefore when a king speaks words of double
meaning, his subjects become distrustful, and
disaffection among friends and hatred among
enemies increase, to such an extent, that in the

end, all the works of the hands, and all the arrows of design from the palm of the hand, having fled forth, are cast to the winds.

36. A king reading books of morality must pay attention to the instructions; and paying attention to these things, the more good discussions and inquiries take place, the more advantageous it is, because, the things of morality and instruction are, as it were, a cultivation, and discussion is, as it were, water, and the more water there is in the cultivation the more prosperous will it be.

37. The more a king's dominions increase, the more must he grow in worthiness and affability himself; the more his dignity rises, the more is it his wisdom to increase his courtesy; but if, when his dignity rises, instead of politeness, pride and haughtiness increase, friends will dislike him and enemies despise him.

38. It becomes a king every morning and evening to notice attentively the bright sun of the high heavens; how, notwithstanding his infinite splendour and majesty, he becomes weak

every evening and sets beneath the earth. In like manner should a king keep always the thought of the rise and fall of his country and dominions in his heart; and as that sun in his short career bestows many advantages on this earth by his light, so the king, by doing good and righteous works, should endeavour to keep his subjects happy and contented.

39. Two qualifications are necessary in a king; first courage, and secondly a majestic bearing, so as to command respect and homage; for by courage he can overcome difficulties, and bring back together his estranged friends; and by a majestic bearing he can disperse his assembled enemies and avert calamities.

40. A king in the time of peace should always lift up the hand of liberality, and in the time of war a hand wielding a sword; for by the former he obtains an increase of friends, and by the latter a diminution of enemies.

41. It becomes a king to keep in his hand by affection and kindness, the hearts and tongues of the upper classes, that is of the great and

rich among his subjects; for these can keep in restraint the tongues, hearts, and hands, of the classes beneath them; as nobody attends to the cawing of the crow, but all hear the song of the nightingale.

42. The best guardian of the life and dignity of a king is his property and treasure. A king is, as it were, a light, and his property a moth. As a moth lays down his life for the light, so all wealth and property can be destroyed for the safety of the king. The treasures of the king's friends are, as it were, a sword which possesses power to fight for the king or to withstand the attack of the king's enemies.

43. As long as a king does not open the mouth of his purse, so long will he continue unable to collect an army. As long as the light does not shine in an assembly, so long will the moths not make their appearance.

44. To act unjustly towards friends is the same in effect as doing a service to enemies.

(Counsels in metaphoric verses.)

Consider that to be the best of all dispositions, which hates evil and pride of every sort.

Thread burns brightly when associated with wax; as is the company, so is the result.

Do not be off thy guard with a silent enemy; an earthquake may succeed a calm, and destroy country, houses, and palaces.

With the weak, rebellion is considered foolish: bottles striking a brass vessel will obtain no advantage.

Those in whom is perfection do not make unnecessary noise; the full moon does not demand the admiration of man.

Burning lamps teach the lesson that they who lift up their heads will be consumed like their wicks.

Never consider any one inferior to thyself; in a dark night a small light is of more service than a great stick.

Do not be proud of thy ancestry: the image in the mirror will never be considered a man.

Do not cast an evil eye upon the fallen: the dust when it rises goes up to the heavens.

Humility is the best accompaniment of a high position: the dust even goes flying up to the

16 A

heavens, but the bubble that lifts up its head with haughtiness, becomes utterly annihilated by the slap of the waves.

Do not cast a contemptuous look upon the weak : a weak thread may bind together hundreds of diamonds and roses.

Do not consider it discreditable to sympathise with the state of the helpless : a precious pearl gives grace to a thread.

A mean man will become proud on obtaining a high position : there is more noise in the upper story than below.

Never consider any work a secret : God knows the secrets and mysteries of every heart.

That person obtains the rest of both the worlds, who, while continuing affable towards an enemy, loves a friend.

Companionship with the wicked makes the good bad : by the company of fire, wood becomes fire.

He who makes a show of his own strength is, as it were, painting a picture on running water.

The water of a flood does not by raging become a sea, so the straight road never suggests itself to a violent man.

If thy state here be exalted, better the condition of the weak.

As no sugar is required in a mother's milk, so when there is a flow of love between two, no outward show of honour and respect is necessary; the mutual love of the hearts is enough.

According to their necessities all receive sustenance from God; a fly comes into the web of a spider.

As there is no rose tree without thorns, so no creature exists here without troubles.

The affection of every thing is set on its own species, if straws see amber they are attracted towards it.

Were a stupid man even to sew up his eyes in a book, yet would he not see, even dimly, the true meaning.

An empty brain cannot think right thoughts; a bubble cannot know the extent of the sea.

The needy do not obtain their desire from the hard-hearted; the polish of a knife imparts no lustre to the face of a knife-sharpening machine.

Crooked things can never, by force, become straight; a bent bow can never become an arrow.

The pen may write ever so much every moment, but it has no power to understand the meaning; so a person who has an empty brain will expend his efforts and thoughts in vain.

From the laughing of the rose this voice is heard, " The heart of that man blooms who holds forth golden hands."

Like the needle of the compass be thou a guide; taking pains thyself, seek the happiness of others.

Dying is very dreadful to the rich, as it is very difficult to walk backwards.

A wicked man cannot keep faithful for many days; the dregs of wine soon became separate from the pure liquor.

Like the pieces of chess, life passes away here unseen; but as the empty squares of the board remain, so also do evil works remain in the memory.

Do not pick faults in a great man, for if thou send forth thy arrow to the heavens, it will only return and wound thee.

The grief of slander never touches the hearts of the pure; from necessity a wise man becomes a companion of his enemy, as a pointless pen makes love with a knife.

A man of many thoughts becomes distracted, as a bow slacked through over much use, is only fit to become the bow of a cotton cleaner.

When one road is shut up ten are opened, as a dumb man makes hundreds of gestures.

As the character of a tree is known by its fruits, so by the son the principles of a father are displayed.

Silence is unlawful to the man who, by moving his tongue, may be a help to the whole world.

As a black hair is easily seen in milk, so people see at once a fault in a good man.

The careless are not made vigilant by strictures of the tongue, as a deadened foot does not care for a thorn.

If thou wishest to keep thy body and mind prosperous, extinguish, as with water, the fire of thy anger.

The senseless man who, in order to increase gold, takes much trouble, decreases by it his own years.

With a shut mouth thou wilt be like a fragrant bud, an open mouth brings trouble to the garden of the soul.

Ridicule is as the fire of separation, reverence is as the water of the life of friendship.

From an ignorant man do not expect a shut mouth, as thou wilt not find empty bottles sealed.

The juice of the honey of silence is so sweet that a wise man's lips stick together by its taste.

When the burden in the womb of a woman increases, to bend low becomes difficult to her, so when the mean man becomes filled with gold, he forgets the practices of respect and reverence.

By heat green fruit becomes ripe, but he who is naturally wicked and of base metal, by the heat of affection becomes all the more vile.

As nothing is joined by scissors, so the grace of union cannot be obtained by a quarrelsome man.

As, although sour vinegar is obtained from wine, but wine can never come out of vinegar, so a man by nature vile, can never become pure, if a hundred years be wasted upon him.

If thou wilt mix with hundreds of maunds of the sugar of affection one bitter word, the effect of that one word will never be removed.

As a diseased eye is pained by light, so when a rash man keeps company with a wise one, his heart is exceedingly grieved, and he considers a wise man a veritable plague.

As water cannot remove the dust from its own face, so he who removes the difficulties of others endures sometimes such sufferings that all means and plans for relieving himself are in vain.

The splendour of him who patiently carries on beneficial works, shines like the sun; and the report of his virtue spreads every where; from east to west he is exalted.

It in a becoming way thou wilt maintain thy own position, thou wilt endure little evil in the world.

Take thy measures before the occurrence of any event; for after the event sighs and groans will be in vain.

As every jot (or point) is read in its proper place, so all wise people heartily prefer each word in its proper season.

If thou hast no natural gift in thee, be thou not proud of the name of thy father.

As there is true natural brightness in the sun, he has no desire for any other light; so those who have true pearls (richness of intellect) do not wish for borrowed ornaments.

As the hook falls into the mouth of a fish, so will the hook of disgrace still the tongue of him who raises objections by crooked arguments; and all the wise will despise him.

In the company of the wicked the good are blamed, as a bitter almond makes even sugar bitter.

The sweat of shame cannot wash away the spot of vice; base sins will not be washed away by weeping.

The garden of this world will not become empty; if one plant passes away another rises.

Such are the water and air of the field of the worldly conduct of mankind, that to-day's sowing becomes ready for reaping to-morrow.

An ignorant man may apply hundreds of maunds of surma to his eyes, yet will he not see the way of wisdom.

Should an ignorant man talk largely of wisdom let not this astonish thee ; for the sleeping one sometimes considers himself awake, and in sleep has thoughts and imaginations.

There are three sorts of friends, the one loving thee with his tongue, one loving thee for thy substance, and one loving thy soul. Never call to thy house the man fond of pleasing thee by talking ; to him who loves thee for thy substance give bread, and bid him farewell; but care for the lover of thy soul with all thy heart ; spend for his sake thy possessions and property.

An avaricious man is not satisfied with both the worlds, as the inside of a bubble is not filled by the sea.

Every thing taken moderately is felt good, a long dress looks all the better by being shortened.

In thy friendship be as a butterfly ; be steadfast to thy friend as he is to the light.

According to all the words written in the book of fate, the affairs of the world happen one after another; one breath having come out, another goes in, and if one comes in the other passes out.

When a mean man finds trust reposed in him he sputters like a wick on which water has fallen; and like it, after much wild flickering, he becomes at last black ashes.

Learning in a self-willed stubborn man is like a light in a stinking privy.

The world closes its eyes upon a thousand virtues, but at one fault it barks like a dog.

In every man therefore these four qualifications are required: first, to be liberal in works of beneficence; secondly, not to grieve the heart of a good friend, for the heart of a friend is like a polished mirror, in which all things will appear exact to thee; thirdly, never to let loose an evil tongue, lest thou have to ask forgiveness, and to repent with grief; fourthly, never to return evil to any who does evil to thee.

If he ask forgiveness of thee, forget his evil, and cleanse thy heart from its remembrance.

Though thou hadst a hundred tongues like a comb, yet shouldst thou never divulge to any one the story of thy secrets.

Engage in no business without the counsel of a friend; do not go to an unknown country by an unknown road.

17 A

It is useless to do a work after the time for doing it has been lost, as after the body is gone the shadow of Homa is unavailing.

As a lamp does not become envious by seeing the sun, so if thou obtain as much as thou needst, be thankful.

As every bird possesses wings and feathers, but there is no power of flying in the wings and feathers themselves, so mere possessions are of no use; a man of possessions must exert himself.

As the particles of the black smoke of a lamp from afar settle on white cotton, so is there jealousy in a black-hearted man; he sticks a false charge to a man of pure heart.

When small dust flies off from the earth, the eyelids instantly cover the bright eyes, so when a base man rides upon a horse, the eyes beholding him with contempt close themselves upon him.

As in order to heal a wound the ashes of a scorpion are used, so sometimes by the wicked, wickedness is remedied.

A man of base origin does not come to give help in difficulty, the toes of the feet cannot loosen tight knots.

As a deadly sword is not made from gold, so in a pure man revenge and malice are not found.

As a straight tooth, having become crooked and making the mouth uncomfortable, is speedily drawn out with pincers, so if any one's son becomes evil he should be immediately driven out from the house.

Inherent vice cannot be removed by the company of the good; by the water-like lustre of glass dust cannot be washed from the face.

As the ill-savoured asafœtida is not improved by rose-water, so neither can the horns of the deer bloom under the influence of spring.

If any one's gold be more than his need, consider him truly miserable.

The vices of a man of low birth cannot be diminished; as the teeth of a snake are not made harmless by biting.

There is no one conversant with the coming events of this world; no one is wise enough to read the writing of fate.

He who is slandered walks straight, as a crooked file gives straightness to other things.

As the dew on the rose does not become rose-water, so in the company of the good, a bad man does not become noble.

As the sea does not tell the value of its pearls, so a virtuous heart does not proclaim its own virtues.

Those who are of hard hearts cannot be softened by affection: if heated iron be left alone for a moment it will become hard iron again, a thousand different means might be employed upon it in vain.

A rich miserly man can never be a hearty friend of an unfortunate man; the poisonous serpent dwelling in a cell sits upon treasures and licks the dust.

As a picture of a lion painted on a wall, so, harmless, should be the dread of a king.

As a lamp does not give light near its own foot, and the light of another lamp is required there; so a man does not see his own defects, but must gain a knowledge of them from another.

An able man has no fear for his livelihood; the key of a livelihood is in the claw of a lion.

Let a nail be of gold or of diamond, but nobody puts it in the eye; so a base man may be extremely handsome in appearance, yet great men do not make friendship with him.

As in the company of pearls the thread remains quite distinct, so do bad men if they enter into the company of the good.

Happy is the man who always abstains in this world from two evil things; who does not take a bad wife, even though she be a fairy, and does not grasp gold in his hand even though it were promised to last to the judgment day.

If thou wishest to have the pearls of wisdom, or to sweep away the filth of ignorance from thy heart, then adorn thy body with these three things, little food, little sleep, and little speech.

A flatterer will not be faithful to thee; the cane plant cannot yield sweet fruits.

A wise man first employs forethought, the word that is gone cannot return to the mouth again.

A man who is naturally senseless do thou with thy knowledge consider to be a book with an imposing title, outwardly attractive, but inwardly worthless.

If thou wilt be a servant of thy teacher, thou wilt speedily become a lord over others.

If thou wishest thy heart to be pure as a mirror, cleanse away ten things from thy heart,— impurity and envy, avarice and slander, pride and enmity, craftiness and oppression, all manner of iniquitous niggardliness, and unlawful revenge. By this thou wilt find grace in both worlds.

Consider not the wrath of great men free from mercy; the thunder of the heavens brings vivifying rains; sometimes words prove treasures by which the troubles of the good and evil are removed.

As rain at the proper season becomes a pearl in the sea, and flowers and leaves on the earth, so when any thing happens in its own time a good effect is produced by it.

A poisonous thorn stuck on a wall gives us this lesson, that if a base man were to sit on a high seat, the mark of greatness would not appear in him.

With the spectacles of wisdom a heart can be read, with the arrow of the sighs of grief stones can be pierced.

The best things to give are rice and pulse, the best not to give is a word of abuse from the mouth; the best to drink is the cup of anger, the best not to eat is unlawful gain.

The friendship of a senseless man is like a glass jug, which being broken with a tap is destroyed.

The friendship a of wise man is a vessel of gold, if it breaks at any time it can be mended again.

If thou wishest to be free from grief in the world, do not get up quarrels with others.

The wicked man is grieved by seeing a heart without revenge, as a black African looking upon a mirror is ashamed.

In courage thou mayst be heroic Rustam, but want will make thee a weak zál (a fox).

After much joy comes much weeping: the laughing of the lightning ushers in the pouring rain.

The hands of the man who is well skilled are like a tree of precious gold, but the hands of the unskilful, in whose mouth are only pompous words, are like the horns of a bull. By the former the whole world is benefited, by the latter their body is greatly pained.

By skill an ill fortune is not changed, a crow cannot by eating bones become a Homa.

As a rose is torn and scattered by a slight breath of air, so a good man by a slight fault feels greatly ashamed.

As only by an axe can wood be cleaved, so only by flogging can a bad man be improved.

As clear eyes are hampered by spectacles, so a bright heart is made obscure by discussion.

It is said that the earth rests upon the horns of a bull; but this fact is true, that he who takes upon himself the burden of the world becomes a bull, he wallows continually in pain and difficulty.

(On Silence.)

If thou wishest thy mouth to be fragrant as
a bud, never remove the fastening of silence.
The diver silently goes into the sea and brings
to hand the truly delectable pearl. In a closed
mouth thou wilt find tranquillity of heart, but
otherwise a rent will form in thy heart, as in
a pen. Do not speak even a little without deli-
beration; do not reply to any body before thou
art asked. Two ears have been given thee and
one tongue, that having heard twice, thou shouldst
speak what is right. Men who appreciate
the pearl of wisdom always give forth true
pearls from their mouth. A speaker of little
will not see shame; one grain of musk is better
than a hundred maunds of dust. Truly wise men
speak as much as is wanted; lofty mountains do
not speak except to reply. As a lock of a box
suggests the thought that there must be in that
box gold or valuables, so of the person to whose
lips a lock is applied people form a high opinion.
If thou wantest a remedy for an impure
mouth, fasten thy lips with the lock of silence.

By prudent speech the treasure of the heart is preserved; by speaking imprudently rebellion rises in the domain of the soul.

(On Youth and Old Age.)

When in the rainy season frequent showers fall, the water in the rivers becomes dirty; so when the spring of man's youth blooms, by perverse conduct he is always defiled. Even in youth perform all good actions, and consider thy black hair as the blackness of a single night. As the pearls of words written with ink are seen through the whiteness of the paper, so in thy old age thou wilt value thy youth. If thou repent of sins in thy youth thou wilt certainly taste more or less of good from it; but in thy old age when thou lose thy teeth, the blessing of repentance will not be delicious to thee. From out of thy sleep old age will suddenly awake thee; thy hair, of the colour of cotton, will be the pillow of death. The blackness of the hair having gone be thou watchful; if, night having gone, morning come,

18 A

be thou awake. By colouring, whiteness of the hair cannot be hidden, by any artifices the fall of the year (Autumn) cannot be made Spring. As hailstones fall from the heavens, so in old age the pearls of the teeth drop down. As the body grows old, hope becomes young; in the hundredth year the tooth of ambition comes up. As at the close of the night there is less brightness in the lamp, so in old age the strength of wisdom decreases. As at the close of the night sleep seems very pleasant, so in old age the dread of death increases. By eating fat, old age does not get strength; as by soaking a bone in butter it will not acquire fatness. A bent back makes signs to the earth old people, as it were, seek out their own graves. When a bad man sees the termination of his life, the face of his heart is painted with streaks of tears. In old age the body will become as a bent sickle; therefore sow in thy youth things worthy to be reaped. When an old man becomes bent as a bow, his eyes do not stay in their place; his steps are not firm, his feet are in his hands, his eyes are in his pockets. As a string of thread comes out from cotton, so from the white hair come forth wishes. From the time when the ice of old age falls upon the head, the fire of youth becomes gradually reduced. A wicked man becomes very careless in age, as the watch-dog of night sleeps during the day. The troubles of old age cannot be removed by gold or valuables ; hundreds of pearls cannot do the work of one tooth. White hair is as it were the enemy of life ; darken the face of this enemy by thy works. Consider old age such a plant that the fruits of death always grow upon it ; consider it good to think on this ; if its fruits are death, what must its thorns be ? When thou art ten or twenty years old do not live carelessly ; till thirty the relish of life will last ; at forty thy body will begin quickly to droop away ; after fifty thou wilt lose thy health, dimness will come to thy eye, and thy whole self will become inactive ; at sixty thy understanding will begin to fail ; at seventy thou wilt be debarred from all labours, when thou art going from eighty to ninety thy throat will swallow less food ; and when thou reachest one hundred or more thy trembling hands will at last be seized by death.

***

(On Prayer.)

Keep thy soul always happy in the world; with joy always remember God. In prayer keep thy mind humble; for lovely flowers grow only from black earth. Worship is the only true duty of youth; do not delay it till old age. He who travels during the black cold night may remain at the stage during the burning sunshine. The drops of dew falling down from heaven engage, like the grains of a rosary, in importunate prayer. The growing fragrant bud of every tree keeps its mouth shut in humility and in remembrance of the Lord. True prayer is an eternal treasure; he is the true man who maintains friendship with the Lord. O son, know that the prayer of midnight will overcome the difficulties of the whole world. So wonderful is the water-splash of prayer that it will quench the calamity of hundreds of consuming fires. By one cold sigh of an earnest midnight prayer the blackness of the world is illuminated. To-day perform thou such acts of worship as to prepare thy goods for travel to-morrow; then with a smiling face thou mayst take thy departure, while others weeping draw out their heart's blood. Never lend thou to a man who does not pray, even though he may rend his hair by reason of the pangs of hunger. He who does not feel his duty to his Creator will never remember thy claims. In prayer let thy heart and tongue be united; with one finger the knot of a string will not be loosened. Shouldst thou remain awake any night for the sake of prayer, the eyes of thy heart will be brightened with an invisible surma.

(On Repentance.)

Consider that to be the worst kind of vice of which thou wouldst remain ignorant to the end. If from the eyes of repentance thou wilt drop a single tear, a cloud of sin having been washed away, thou wilt become pure. As by the scattering of stars in the sky the night becomes (bright as) morning, so the filth of sin is cleared away by tears. Do not remain careless concerning repentance, for the next world will give a pearl in return for thy every tear. If thou keep the eyes of thy heart filled with water, do not be afraid of the fire of hell. O my son, sin is the heritage of Adam, from child to child it has continued to descend. In youth duly do thou the work of repentance, for without teeth the skin of the lips will not be cut. The Lord does the Lord's works, work thou as man. The mercy of the Lord is greater than our sinfulness, therefore it is not necessary that every little particular should be remembered. When the soul becomes bitter with the poison of sin, the medicine of repentance only will suit it. In the courts of the liberal wonderful works of merit are done; for the sake of a drop of water, the sins of a hundred years are forgiven. By weakness only man becomes a sinner, therefore doth that powerful Benefactor forgive him.

CHAPTER VIII.

Prince Albert's dying sickness; the blessing asked by him, and the good counsels given to his eldest son and to Victoria.

COUNSELS of this sort, many and various, one after another, did Albert give to his son. O reader, if there be any understanding in thee, see clearly from hence how the poets give life to the dying, how by mere words of fancy they convey true impressions, how they make one drop a spreading sea, and how from one bud they lay out a garden of roses. Know thou him to be truly foolish who cannot from a sign make out the inner meaning. I have written the whole beginning as above; now hear from me the end of the story. Be not thou sad from hearing it, for such is the way of the revolving earth. In all things the Lord has His purposes;

by Him only good and evil fortune exist. The remedies of all diseases are in His hands; by Him one withers and another flourishes.

In the Christian year 1861, on an evil day of the month of October, Prince Albert and his wife having travelled in Scotland came to London; at this time the good and eminent Albert was not thoroughly well in body, but not minding his pain, he did not take care of himself, and did not take any medicine. He went also to Cambridge to gladden his heart by seeing his son. There he met his eldest son and talked with him earnestly on topics suitable for him. Then he remembered the hunting ground, and prepared the things necessary for it; and with powder and gun, and pistol and sword, he furnished his handsome person. Laying aside his princely apparel he put on that of a hunter; brightness came to his eyes, and thoughts of slaughter to his heart. Like the tiger he wandered in the jungle everywhere, and visited the game with the calamity of bullets. Running and dashing he sent forth shout upon shout, he leaped upwards and downwards, and in all such toils

of hunting the day was spent, and the dark-
coloured evening came. So red did his face become with excitement that it looked from a
distance like the planet Mars; and so filled with
perspiration was his body, that there was flowing from it as it were a sea of priceless pearls.
This fatigued and perspiring body he exposed
for a long time to the open air, so that violent
fever ensued; but he took no advice and drank
no medicine. In this manner several days passed,
and then a review of the army taking place,
he went with the Queen to see it. Suddenly
rain set in; but Albert stood there persistently
for a long time and consequently his former
illness rapidly increased. He lost the whole
strength of his body, a racking pain was felt in
every limb; his back began to break with pain,
his body became hot with fever, like the fire of
a furnace. Then he sought aid from a physician, but when an arrow issues forth from the
bow of Death, the shield of contrivance or wealth
is of no avail. Kings and beggars are equally
destroyed. The physician used means upon
means, but the illness increased in spite of every

19 A

thing that could be done. The virulence of the disease had become so great by the dawn of the next day, that a shout of alarm rose amongst his relatives, and the report of it spread all over London, and high and low became anxious. Learned physicians tried every means in their power, but the root of the strange disease could not be reached. O brother, the body is truly a wonder; whose structure nobody comprehends, the key of whose secrets are in the hands of the Lord, where the eyes of wisdom and of skill are blind. Every moment the disease greatly increased, and on the 14th December 1861 there was great consternation, for the rapid approach of the last breath was manifest. Then in every direction were the electric wires employed. His eldest son had been sent for from Cambridge, and the very moment he arrived by the railway he was made to stand before his dying father. Seeing him, Albert heaved a sigh from his heart, and said :—

O youthful son, continue to be no longer childish, for the high heaven being displeased with me, I abandon this frail world and go. I commit to thee the rule of this house and this country; so behave thyself that my name may endure. With thy good mother continue to be loving; never in the least vex her soul. Do not even for a moment think a thought without God. Never do any thing against His commands. Keep thy hands closed from wickedness; be always seeking the holy Lord. Keep my counsels ever in remembrance." Then he lifted up his hands to heaven and said:—

(*A Prayer.*)

O Benevolent Guide, both the worlds have Thy help and protection; earth is Thy servant, and heaven is subject unto Thee. All crowned kings are in Thy hand. I humbly bow the head of my heart to ask a last favour of Thee for myself. Continue thou the Protector of this my son; be Thou the solver of every one of his difficulties; for by Thee only are the sun, the heavens, and the earth. Thou only art the true friend of the distressed. I have not performed service worthy of Thee; on account of this, shame rests upon the face of my soul. Whatever may be wicked do thou forgive me unasked. With an open heart I make this confession, that sins without number have been here by me committed. From drinking of the cup of carelessness I remained here intoxicated; the bottle of life has fallen from my hands. Clothe me now with the robe of Thy mercy; cause me to drink the wine of Thy wonted forgiveness. Now I travel from hence to my country; be Thou my Guide in the way. O merciful

One, O King, O Creator, O Lord, O Righteous and Majestic One, forgive my sins. When the dust of black darkness falls on my body, show Thou me the light of the lamp of Thy mercy. Do not leave me to the protection of others ; do not leave me to taste the fruits of my own plant. I have no more power to move than a flying straw when stopped by a wall, therefore do Thou bestow on me the grace of Thy love. Draw me to Thy arms as dry straws are drawn by amber.

———∞∘◦⊙◦∘∞———

(*The Blessing given to the Queen.*)

Then he looked towards the beloved of his soul, for the last time opened the lips of love, and spoke words of blessing, such as these :—

" O thou excellent one, life of my soul, never may thou feel the grief of my separation from thee. But shouldst thou be wounded by this grief, there is no other remedy but the balm of resignation ; reign here living as thou hast lived. May thy joy remain ever young. May wealth be the foundation of thy kingdom. May all thy subjects be filled with blessings. May God be thy all-sufficient Guide. May the water of the Lord's mercy abide in the royal garden. May the warmth of the light of justice continue in thy kingdom. May the crowns of emperors be the dust of thy feet. As thy ring holds a diamond, so may thy sense comprehend the secrets of heaven. As long as the heaven and earth endure, so long may thy justice and faith continue. May the fragrant and lovely rose of thy fame bloom day and night by the breath of mercy. May the fortress of prosperity be thy protection here. Be a guardian with all thy heart to these children. Be kind to my poor relations. Accept this last farewell;* forget my negligence, imperfections, and errors; having remained together so long, now we part; having seen many joys now we see sorrows. But all this is the design of the Creator."

---

* For one day before the death of Prince Albert, which occurred on the 14th day of December 1861, at 10-50 P.M., Queen Victoria and her daughter Alice remained with him, and attended to him with heart and soul till the hour of his death, and during this time, his eldest son the Prince of Wales was also present in a very distressed state. The death of her husband occasioned great grief and distress to the excellent Victoria. At such time her daughter Alice administered to her much comfort, with great understanding and resignation; and in this great difficulty she looked after all things with much courage. Unfortunately at the death of Albert all his children were not present.

CHAPTER IX.

The last words spoken by Albert, on the vanity of the things of this world. After this his death, &c.

WHATEVER this frail world gives us it always sooner or later takes back. As a bud in a garden grows with a closed mouth, and having bloomed dies rejoicing; so whoever among mankind is humbly born but at the time of death hears the report of his goodness, is to be considered indeed fortunate, for goodness alone proves efficacious to the end.

Consider the world a prison, from which all who get an excuse go out, and will never again remember it; having gone to another they are happy. As fire does not abstain from burning those who practise fireworship all their lives, so the world never bestows any special favour upon those who bind the heart of their souls to the world. When the honeycomb is filled with honey,

the bees abandon the place and go away, so generally when people are filled with riches the hunter
of death comes and parts them from their riches
suddenly.   Wise men do not like wealth ; as long
as there is a crown on the wick of a lamp, so long
there is sputtering. If the waves of the sea were to
become swords, the empty-hearted bubble would
not care for them, so dervishes do not receive a
wound from gold, they forget their distress in the
enjoyment of contentment.   As a fast-bound bird
cannot soar on high, so a soul tied to the earth
cannot rise to heaven.   Consider this life as a
dream or a shadow, where pain of body and
trouble of spirit are encountered ; where man
only understands any thing after getting hundreds of raps, and when his ears are wrung;
where tyrannical and wicked men are considered
as wolves and foxes and base dogs. If the
world is as a distressing dream, it is better that
the eyes be kept shut there.   A bright-hearted
man keeps aloof from the world, as the light of
a lamp keeps at a distance from the lantern.

While speaking thus the breath of the Prince's
body came to his lips, he went to heaven by an

unseen road, the caged nightingale flew high aloft, forsook an unclean world, and went to the garden of paradise. Upon this the Queen felt such distress that her good sense did not remain with her; her brain turned like a swing with grief, and a fainting dizziness seized her heart; worldly pleasure and rejoicing became disgusting to her. Heaving a sigh she struck her forehead; looking at her children she shed torrents of tears.

(The Consolation given by the Princess Alice.)

This seeing, the Princess Alice said, " O dear mother, never do this; take us children into thy hands; for truly ours is the inestimable misfortune, that we have lost so good a guardian, we are from this day fatherless children.* But now do thou take the place of our father.

---

* As said above, Albert died on 14th December; but this eminent man had given up all hope of his life from the 11th, and when they removed him from his usual place into the palace of George IV. and William IV. where both these sovereigns died, Albert openly began to say that in the hour that was passing he would die; and so it happened. In the great crowd of gentlemen who were round about him at his last hour, there were several Germans, French, Portuguese, and

Now remember thou God in this affliction. Collect thy accustomed patience, do not murmur impatiently in any way. Bow thy head to the Divine will. Consider not His dispensations void of purpose. If these are the mysteries of the will of God, take His afflicting visitation as surma, and with it paint patiently the eyes of thy heart, that the black coloured grief may become bright through its means; for no disadvantage can happen to a child from the chastisement of a father. This world is like a poisonous thorn, those people who put on it the feet of their hearts, are pained and grieved and wounded by it. It is most right that we should be pleased with the things which the Benefactor does; whether His dispensations be grievous, or joyous, no murmuring is seemly in man. As a potter makes every sort of vessel of clay, but there is no power in the clay to ask the potter his reasons, or be so irreverent as to make any murmuring,

---

Englishmen; and having bade a farewell to them in their different languages, he breathed his last. The day before this renowned man died, he had not the power of recognizing people; but he was able to distinguish well, and to the last moment, Her Majesty Victoria.

20 A

so must we consider mankind. No fault-finding with Divine workmanship can be proper. Five different fingers are on the hand of death, and whenever it wishes to do any work it puts two upon the eyes, and two upon the ears, and placing one upon the mouth, it says 'Hold thy tongue.' A holy heart is not distressed by grievous dispensations; the glass of the mirror does not become dim by reason of a grieved countenance. Wise men consider him thoroughly ignorant who is distracted concerning the advent of death. The waves of the sea are not stopped by the hand; trying to stop one, two instantly make their appearance; therefore, O wise-hearted, excellent mother, think thou of the past and of the future." When she heard such words from her daughter, her grief was in a measure allayed. With courage she maintained patience in her heart, and bore her burden for a time.

The news spreads of the death of Prince Albert, and a sad and melancholy sight takes place in consequence, and the ceremony of his burial is performed.

When Albert thus died, the sad news spread over the whole country. At midnight telegraphic messages sped one after another. Lamentation rose in every house and family. The great bell of the church rung,* the noise resembled that of the judgment day. The news of the sad death reached the countries of France, Prussia, Austria, Russia, and Germany. Murmuring and confusion, and lamentation and sorrow, moved from one place to another, mile after mile.

All the ministers and statesmen arrived at the palace, and when night passed away, and the morning light dawned, all things necessary to be done were attended to. Old and young came from distant countries, a crowd of men and women assembled; the veins of the blood of grief flowed in every one's body, sorrowing friends wept every where, for a sad calamity had happened in the joyous palace. All, looking at

---

* In the great church called St. Paul's, there is a bell larger than any other in London, which is never rung on any occasion except when one of the royal family of England dies. The news was given to the inhabitants of the whole city by the ringing of this bell for two hours in the middle of the night.

his face, were surprised. The beautiful body had become soul-less, but his tranquil heart was seen in his placid features. The dead face showed the goodness of his soul, the divine light was seen upon him. The whole city mourned with a sincere heart, and closed their shops, offices, and houses; and the usually thronged streets became deserted. The army bound the sign of mourning upon their persons; all heroes drew blood from the eyes of their hearts; all, high and low, of the city, came together, and put on the black coloured garments of deep mourning. A mantle of grief was, as it were, spread over the earth. When other nobles came from distant countries, it was settled that on the 23rd the body of the deceased should be buried; necessary directions were given, and a box or coffin of everlasting sleep was made ready, worthy of the noble dead; and they placed him in that coffin,* as is the way of all in this world.

---

* It was first thought that three weeks after the day on which the eminent Albert died his body should be buried; but as the sight of the corpse of this highly blessed man occasioned excessive grief and despondency to the good Queen Victoria, which perchance would tend to the injury of

According to royal custom this coffin con-
sisted of four boxes and covers, one within
the other, of which the first box and cover
were of smooth polished ebony, the second was
of lead, the third was a box of still thicker ebony,
the fourth had a cover of silver and superior crimson velvet embroidered together; and upon this
box his name, with particulars of his age and
descent, were all described in detail. At the head
of this an engraved silver crown was attached;
at its foot were placed in silver the arms corresponding with all the titles the deceased had;
and in the middle part, upon a large silver
plate, was engraved his titles.

When the 23rd day came, all the people assembled there sorrowing, all the ceremonies were
performed according to the customs of the coun-

---

her health, the ministers consulting with each other fixed
upon the 23rd December for the funeral. By this time the
friends and acquaintances who were to come from distant
countries arrived; and the Duchess of Wellington and the
Duchess of Sutherland, two ladies of high position, stayed with
the good Victoria many days to console her and to make her
forget her grief; and they endeavoured to lessen her overwhelming distress by speaking constantly words of counsel
and of wisdom.

try and religion; and the whole community walked along lamenting. Upon all the rose trees grew the thorns of grief; the blooming cypresses became as yellow hay. Over whatever dust the body of the deceased moved it flew up, with a cry of grief, to the heavens. In the cold season arose the fire of intense grief. The nightingales, forgetting their singing, cried out like crows. The beasts of the forest wept bitterly; lions and leopards forgot their prey in their grief. The heart of all England was pained and scarred; faces like the pomegranate flower became pale.

O brother, though thou be a lord of this world, thou wilt not find any thing save a narrow place, two or three feet broad and eight feet long; and finally leaving that, thou wilt become invisible. Observe this drama before thy eyes. What palaces Albert had, of how many cities and villages he was lord; but after death what did that good man obtain? When they reached St. George's chapel* they took the corpse into it, where a cell was ready, near which past kings

---

* There are vaults for laying up the royal corpses in a place named St. George's Chapel, Windsor. In these vaults there

slept; and there they caused Albert to take his last rest. Abandoning this world he left behind him a good name. Such are the workings of heaven, wise men never make any claim upon or war with it. This creation thus rolls along. Here we experience joy and sorrow. One goes first, another follows; but dry dust is the end of them both. Such is the course of this world, it has no youth, it has no age. Whether thou art a beggar or a king, thou wilt get after death one torn sheet. Thou wilt find a place solitary and dark; there wilt thou be reminded of thy doings. There thou wilt surely find terror or joy; thou wilt meet there with strict justice only. In the hand of the great hunter of this revolving heaven,

---

are two sets of cells, in one of which the corpses of the royal family of Hanover are placed; the second is set apart for those who die as sovereigns of England. The corpse of the eminent Albert was placed among the latter. There was a custom of lighting lamps and candles while burying the royal corpses in this manner, but this custom was given up after the burial of King William IV., therefore at the time of the burial of Albert no lamp was lighted. At the time of the funeral procession the Prince of Wales, the eldest son of the deceased, walked first as the chief mourner, and he was followed by the Duke of Cambridge, the Prince of Prussia (son-in-law of Victoria), and others.

there is a noose so extensive that it falls upon the neck of every soul indiscriminately, and none is free from its grasp. This world is, as it were, an iron chain, the young or old who break through this chain will win a fort of gold in the next world, and will be filled completely with happiness of body and mind. Country and property, children and wife, will stay with thee till thou art buried; sorrowing relatives will remain behind, but none will become dust with thee. This existence is soon followed by non-existence; keep firm the stirrups of the horse of thy soul; cast away the banner of avarice from thy hand; keep tight the reins, because the horse is lame. Surprising are the affairs of this world, do not put thy trust in any thing. Do not be deceived and caught in the snare, for evil always remains behind the veil. Tossing up and down continue here; one rises high and the other falls low. In one minute one comes, and another passes away. He who will feel himself here as dead while he lives, will live after death. Those who weep with grief in dread of death, throw as it were bitter rose-water into sugar.

The world is like a pit of miry clay, the greater weight thou place upon it the deeper thou wilt sink. How long shall we go on with such conversation? the cotton of inattention is in the ears of the people.

CHAPTER X.

Verses describing the effect wrought by separation on true
loving and beloved ones, &c.

The shadow of the head, in the prime youth,
Departed from this place ;
The treasure of my heart being robbed,
My weight and value in the world are lost.
O, my beloved has departed from me,
His sign is nowhere to be seen ;
A tortured body has he left behind,
And carried the precious soul with him.

A Jesus-like form has become invisible,
Then what hope is there now for the dead !
When the bright lamp has been extinguished
Why should the moth longer stay ?
Is there any such messenger here,
Who would speed to the land of non-existence,
Who, with a tongue delicious as honey,
Would give this message to my beloved ?—

The nightingale of the garden,
With thy fragrance is greatly intoxicated ;
For thy face, with open eyes,
The roses are anxiously waiting.

O light of my eyes do thou come,
Because for thy heart-charming face,
I have, like the flower of narcissus,
Reserved a place in mine eyes.

How much to see thy face this my soul thirsteth;
If thou wert to know aright,
Thou wouldst bring a sea of tears with thee.
The bud of the hope of my heart,
A cold sigh now causes to wither,
And with the fire of separation
My body is scorched like kubab.

Come thou soon, come O lover,
For the glad season of spring is departing;
That we may drink the wine of love,
For the rose garden is fully prepared.
In anxious waiting for thy face
The pupil of my eye comes forth;
Appear thou openly or secretly,
That I may find " munsookh "* and rest.

(2.)

O God be gracious unto me,
Give heed to my loneliness,
For without the beloved the heart is lifeless;
Hear Thou my complaint.
From the cage of this world, if the bird
That has suddenly flown
Were to show his face but a moment,
The age that has gone would return.

---

* The word " munsookh," elsewhere rendered peace of
mind, a happy mind, &c., occurring in the last of each of the
sets of verses from this place to the end, I have thought better
to preserve untranslated.—*Translator's Note.*

The eyes of this heart are fixed
Upon the nest of his face only,
Do Thou graciously bring him,
For these eyes are his only dwelling place.
The lover, the dust of whose feet
Was the crown of my head,
Keep not away from me, that I may
Enjoy this kingdom with "munsookh."

(3.)

To whom shall I tell the grief of my heart ?
There is no sympathizer here.
Without thee, O my beloved,
There is no helper here.
As in the double kernel of the almond,
There is a gaping wound in my breast ;
If thou wert to show thy face for a moment
This my wound would be healed.

Like the bright moon of the second day
I stand bending my body,
That if I see thy sunlike face
I might seize thee and embrace thee.
O rosebud-mouthed possessor of my heart,
Though I am so straitened with grief,
Yet live I still without thee,
And my soul is considered as hard as stone.

Come thou, O beloved one, come ;
Though my senses are scarified,
Yet these mine eyes will recognize thee,
Thou only desire of my soul !
I stand in thy way like the dust,
Burning in body and mind,
Throw thou the shade of thy feet upon me,
That I may find "munsookh" a little.

(4.)

In thy grievous separation to-day's day even
Has fled into night,
In the expectation of meeting thee
Soon my whole life will be ended.
Oh, waiting and expecting thee,
The pupil of the eye of this soul
Is tired and dropping out ;
Bestow upon it but one single thought.

By intoxication of wine, by atar of roses,
Or the bright pearl of the shell,
There is no such telling effect,
As there is on my heart through thee.
Come thou here to me secretly,
That I may hide from both the worlds.
In power, in wealth, in throne, and in crown,
I have no delight, but in thee !

(5.)

The season of spring has come again ;
In this lovely garden,
Sweet nightingales are warbling songs,
In remembrance of the sweet smelling rose.
If thou go from here to the place of my beloved,
O breeze, that causest blooming and fruit-bearing,
Bestow on him countless blessings,
Of leaves and fruits and flowers.

Now a great joy has come
Amongst the people of the world.
The narcissus cups are filled to the brim,
In admiration of thy face.

Like the eyes of a sick body,
So have mine eyes become colourless;
Rubbing, rubbing, wherever I go,
There appears all blackness and dimness.

Come thou, for without the rose of thy face
This lovely spring is sad.
Like infants deprived of milk,
The hearts of buds and fruits are thirsty.
O wipe thou these my brimful eyes
With the skirt of the heart of "munsookh."
Upon the lips of this my parched life,
By sweet words sprinkle water.

(6.)

Without seeing the face of the beloved,
The soul does not care for the world.
Whoever has no beloved in the world,
He is unworthy of honour.
Sing not, O birds of the garden,
Your lovely songs, as David.
For the Solomon of the rose of London
Has this night left love, and departed!

O heart-charming cypresses,
Display not your beauties and graces;
For the beloved dove, carrying the breach of Peace,
Has disappeared suddenly.
There is not wanted, O moon,
The lustre of thy bright disc,
For towards thy country, on his journey,
Has my lover from hence departed!

Since my friend has not remained here,
What shall I do with gold and possessions?
With the wealth of his companionship
My body and soul were quite filled.

A rose in the hand, a cup to the mouth,
And the blessing of a beloved in the arms,
Whatever poor man enjoys,
Know his state to be better than a king's.

To meet thee, O excellent lover,
I am so exceedingly anxious,
That with the rose-coloured pearls of the heart,
My face and my skirt I keep filled ;
That the moment I see thy face,
I may lavish those pearls upon thee,
And make thee sit with love
Upon the eyes of this precious soul.

That woman sees a heaven here
Who enjoys the happiness of a husband ;
But she who loses her husband in youth,
Endures the pains of hell.
If the light of thy sunlike face
Should be reflected upon this moon,
Then in the black heaven of my state,
A star of good fortune would shine.

The moonshine is so bright to-night,
As to cheer even black grief.
From the sieve, as it were, of the heavens,
On all sides pearls are scattered.
But without thee, O heart-soothing lover,
How can I value all this ?
Through my great distress for thy separation,
A sheet is spread over all things.

Bring, O breeze of dawn,
The news of the abode of my beloved,
That seeing the garden of his face
We may cull the roses from the garden of " munsookh."

(7.)

The griefs of love should be asked of a nightingale,
The excellencies of a lovely face
Should be asked of a rose.
Love is like a wilderness
Where birds of the heart miss their way,
Where with the wind of separation,
The sighs of grief fly as black dust.

O wise man, consider love to be the only true alchemy,
Where the dust of this body burns,
And the clear soul becomes pure gold.
As ripe fruits, dropping from the branch,
Fall upon the ground,
So of love that has ripened and is lost,
The result is companionship with the dust.

The man, of whose heart
Love becomes the master in this world,
Takes sighs for his pen
And anxieties for his writing book.
By cold counsels,
The burning of the grief of love is not lessened,
As in the wintry season
The flame of a burning fire is not diminished.

As in the flames of fire, babul and aloe wood burn alike,
So in the field of love,
Men of high and low degree resemble each other.
When the noose of love falls secretly upon the mind,
The veins of the body become chains,
And tie down heart and soul.

As glass being melted becomes water,
And then does not care for a stone,
So he whose heart is melted in love
Does not give ear to counsels.

When the fire of the lightning of love
Falls on the field of the heart,
It burns and consumes to ashes
All kinds of contrivances.

Who, like the wick of a burning lamp,
From the head to the sole of the foot,
Will continue filled with sighs and tears,
He only can obtain the delights of love.
As is the case with a lighted candle,
Calamities fall on a lover at night,
He complains with his tongue, he burns in his heart,
And sheds the blood of his body through his eyes.

As the wick of a yet sinking lamp
Can be ignited in a moment,
So in a heart that has seen grief
Love takes effect with readiness.
As the coolness of the face of Joseph
Burnt Zuleika in the fire,
So love is such a wonderful thing,
That, if water be in one, flame rises in the other!

From the beginning of time
The wide sea of love has been raging ;
In the storm of this sea only
Are both worlds involved every moment.
It is the nature of all swords to cut things in twain ;
But wonderful is the sword of love,
That it joins together two separate things!

In the distressing separation from his beloved
The lover trembles with fever,
As the quicksilver of the earth, which shakes everlastingly.
As a dead body is cast on one side by the sea,
So dead hearts void of love
Are not loved by the merciful Lord.

22 A

As a light that is just going out
Is revived by a slight touch of fire,
So is a dying heart quickened
By the bright flame of love.
If in the path of pure love
My heart is a target for a brave man's arrow,
Then all my contrivances for shielding it are vain.

Weeping, weeping in love for thee,
I have washed away " munsookh" and am weak.
The pupils of mine eyes are always wet,
And are swollen like bubbles.

(8.)

In separation from thee, beloved,
For a long time I am crying,
I draw out from mine eyes tears, resembling pearls,
Whither shall I go to see thee, O lover, now I do not know
In thy very search last night I found myself fallen asleep.

Then in the midst of seeing something wonderful,
The water of lamentation was sprinkled upon my face,
And my delightful dream fled from me!
In the rosary of this world
The lover has business with fire only,
And by internal burning
His face becomes wholly of the colour of ashes.

Besides the bitter breath of sighs,
There is no other breeze in this garden!
In the season and freshness of full spring,
The stalks of the plants are withered.
In the delightful science of music,
The nightingale is considered an Aflatoon,*
But in the school of true love he learns only the alphabet.

* That is, *a philosopher*, as Aflatoon or Plato.

In the lovely spring of youth sad calamities suddenly came,
Body, "munsookh," and all, withered,
And made my soul truly miserable.

(9.)

God knows what is written in my fate.
What has happened I know, but what may still be hidden !
By grief for thee, O lover,
A fire burns in the house of my heart.
Happiness, beauty, riches, possessions,
Burning day and night, become ashes.

In the net of love I am like a bird imprisoned in a cage.
I have such burning sighs
That at last the cage will be consumed.
My years pass away as with death, though I am alive,
The sleep of insensibility lies upon my mind
As the hard stone upon a grave.

Wonderful, wonderful, O heart-possessing man,
That, though a mountain of grief has sat upon my heart,
Yet comes a cold sigh forth !
And my soul is absorbed only in thy remembrance ;
The ground of this thirsty heart
Drinks only the water of tears,
There, on the trees of sighs, grow spark-like fiery fruits.

Of this my burning heart, when the smell comes forth,
The neighbours, amazed,
Inquire where burns this spitted kubab ?
As, in order to mend what is torn,
The thread puts its tongue into the mouth of the needle,
So, O absent beloved one, know thou all my exertions.

For to the cleft that is made in this heart
By the wound of thy separation !
I apply with the skill I possess,
The clasp of the wire of anxiety.

What shall I say of my grief for thee !
My heart has become blood,
My blood has been turned into water,
And this water has washed away " munsookh,"
And come forth by the way of mine eyes.

(10.)

O thou hidden cypress,
Why rememberest thou not the garden ?
Having been the companion of the rose,
Why makest thou not thy heart fragrant ?
Hear, O brothers, hear you ;
For of a distracted mind and broken heart
A hundred fragments as of glass
Are lying in the garden of this body.

Here, from the burning of grief,
The breast glitters like a beautiful rosary,
But even in roses will not be found
Such clefts and cuts as in this.
This nightingale, maddened with the phrenzy of passionate
    love,
Builds its nest of thorns,
And burns all into dust with sighs !

Being without thee, involuntarily I mourn as a flute,
And hold fast with both my hands
The reins of the horse of passion.
When thou camest in my sleep I woke up startled :
Having seen, as it were, the face of the sun,
I woke from my slumbers.

The painful sigh at the dawn, casts fire like the sun,
In a moment it consumes the stones
In the depths of the earth, into ashes.
The recollection of thy curled locks encircling my neck,
Tying down all ease and " munsookh,"
Throws the noose of death upon my soul.

(11.)

My breath comes forth,
But my expectation comes not to pass.
Alas, that my fortune does not take
Some auspicious form.
O my beloved, thy absence brings forth
Sighs from my heart,
As an extinguished lamp causes the wick
To emit black-coloured smoke.

Come, for on account of separation from thee,
These eyes, weeping through the night,
Like running wounds, do not close themselves in sleep.
As by much rain being rained
A clearness appears in the clouds,
It is strange that the dimness of mine eyes
Does not pass away by my constant weeping.

If thou, my Joseph-like lover, wert to come,
Mine eyes would be ready to welcome thee,
But in them now are pits and hollows
As in the cities of Canaan.
With the fire in my heart
My countenance burns in thy remembrance,
Black scars have fallen on my body
Like the marks on the tulip.

Do not do any thing to cause me
To shut the doors of hope in mine eyes,
For only in the expectation of seeing thee,
They remain open, being painted with *surma*.
The sad soul comes now and again to the lips,
And then goes back again.
O God! without Thee, what soul
Can recover lost " munsookh " ?

(12.)

The plant of love having broken and fallen,
The fruits of hope are destroyed;
The branch of distress is grafted here,
And gives pain both day and night.
Hear, O lover, gone afar, that these mine eyes expend
Every day a large sea, but they never borrow from any one.

The hands of these two small black pupils are so free,
That liberality like that of Hatim *
Yields altogether before them.
By the heaving of my heart this breast is always restless,
As the sea becomes ruffled by the leaping of the fishes.

A drop of blood from my heart to-day came,
And stood upon these eyes,
But when it bent to see thy face
That moment it fell and died.
O friends, bestow kindness upon this grieved soul,
Rend this breast with a dagger
And take the heart out from it.

The life of this world is like vain painting upon the water
Wise men enjoying " munsookh" consider life as a bubble.

(13.)

My heart considers no other theme
Save that of thy remembrance!
I give it counsel every way but it will not hear any thing.
On account of thy separation
Every hair of my eyelashes burns like a lamp.
Wonderful lamps do people behold,
On the banks of the streams of running water.

---

* An Arabian chief, proverbial for liberality.

By the red water of the heart
This eyelash had become like blood,
To-day I saw in the sea of these eyes
A branch of red coral.
Without thee truly I sleep,
But my sighs heave and continue wakeful,
Like a dead body lying upon the ground,
And a fiery lamp burning beside it.

As a weak and aged father
Complains in vain of a disobedient son,
So my soul pains itself exceedingly
By heaving sighs to no purpose.
Looking out for thee, O lover,
The hairs of my eyelashes prick my eyes,
As the skirt of a garment is pierced
By the points of poisonous thorns.

I know not whether, through grief for thee,
It is the heart that burns, or the liver,
But from both there comes forth a bad smoke incessantly.
Weeping, lamentation, beating of the breast,
And death, pertain to a lonely lover.
The " munsookh" of that woman is destroyed who loses
    her lover in youth.

(14.)

A long time has passed, O possessor of my heart,
And yet have no tidings come from thee.
Not a verbal salaam has come,
Nor has any written message arrived ;
In my great love for thee this my heart is restless.
The veins and arteries of my body
Are like quivering quicksilver.

O lover, a rent has been made in my heart through grief,
When mending it, the point of the needle
Causes blood to flow.
This distracted heart does not discriminate
Between friend and foe,
When the fire rises in flames,
It burns water and oil alike.

In assemblies of lovers
There are no breasts without scars,
As a hoondi (bill) is not honoured
By any shroff without a seal or a sign.
The remembrance of thy graces and attractions
Destroys this my heart ;
O God ! stay this heart,
For it burns my skin, and mind, and body.

Wise "munsookh" like men
Tear the pages of the book of the heart into shreds,
For in this book of a worldly heart
There never was any thing good.

(15.)

The nightingale takes in its beak
The leaves of the rose
And destroys them,
Singing of thy separation, it weeps in torrents.
In a vision of this world I saw
A vivid representation of the judgment.
First, I saw heaven, and afterwards the depths of hell.

I wish to draw sobs and sighs
In the assembly of the afflicted ;
As long as there is breath in me, as in a flute,
So long I wish to complain.

I have kept this body erect
With the stay of the rod of sighing,
If I cease to breathe forth sighs,
The house of this body will give way altogether.

When I apply to the scars of this heart
The soft cotton-like plasters of counsel,
They are ignited with the fire of my heart,
And make the ghastly wounds fresh within me.
By the thorns of the grief of a lover
I was wounded at every pore,
I was a well-wisher of his, with " munsookh,"
But am now considered his bitter enemy.

(16.)

My heart and my religion
Have gone with thee, my golden one,
Thou hast taken away the golden strength of my soul,
How then shall I remain alive ?
Sight is not able to go beyond the door of mine eye,
Ever since thou, dear-hearted charmer, hast gone,
It has become diseased.

If thou say I will come in thy sleep,
It will prove of no advantage,
For from the day thou hast been separated
There has been no sleep for me.
On the road of thy thoughts
My sight and my heart so run,
That from my brimful eyes blisters rise upon my feet.

Thy separation always scatters
The fire of grief in my heart,
The pupil of my eye shines from a distance
Like the bright burning lamp of the night.

23 A

See, upon this tearful face,
The spray of the waves of a storm.
See, upon this scarred breast,
The crimson roses of the garden.
As from the body of the thorn
The pollen of the rose drops,
So every drop from my grieved heart,
Falls from these eyelashes.
If I refrain from weeping for a moment,
The lamps of mine eyes would be put out,
Fate has so decreed that they
Should retain brightness only in water.

Now cloud, now rain, and afterwards a sprinkling;
Come and see the fountain of the eye,
How it weeps, being deprived of " munsookh."

(17.)

The breeze put me in remembrance yesterday
Of the journey of my friend,
I give my heart also to the breeze, happen what may.
The sockets of these eyes
Have become empty of their pearls of tears,
And this, these eye-lashes make known,
Pointing to a distance with fingers.

Until the scar of love becomes old,
Its goodness is not seen,
As a newly-lighted lamp
Does not shine forth with full lustre.
Tears flowing from a heated heart
Have taken away the strength of my soul,
Half its strength has turned to fire, and half to water.

The broken heart having become despairing,
Sends forth its hidden secrets,
How can it be that a breaking bottle
Will not make a noise ?

By hope only does every thing seem sweet ;
Quench not hope,
For by destroying the store of hope
Thy own value will be still more lessened.

(18.)

Come and flit about this garden, come soon, O nightingale,
Come and see with thine eyes
How the roses of these scars have bloomed.
Thy place is upon the cypress, mine is in the heart,
Who then is here truly miserable ? tell me, O nightingale.

Thou dwellest in the arms of roses, I remain far and alone,
Then see, whether thou or I am in affliction,
See this, O nightingale.
On thy neck is a circle of feathers,
On mine is a chain of iron,
Whose lover is the more cruel ? tell me, O nightingale.

Every morning by thy plaintive strains
Thou bringest great grief upon me,
Thou dost send out fire from thy mouth,
And I burn in the heart, O nightingale.
The true happiness of the world
Is the sweet happiness of a lover.
Without a lover there is no " munsookh,"
But misery ; know thou this, O nightingale.

(19.)

Bedecked in what joyous colours,
Hath the spring come upon us to-day,
The moon shines, the breeze blows,
The flowers and trees are blooming.
If to-day's new day were to cause the earth to bloom,
What profit would there be to me ?
For without a lover, my existence is altogether destroyed.

Beholding the fiery colour of roses, my blood boils greatly,
Like the wick of a burning lamp
Every bud scorches my heart.
The fragrant and lovely coloured spring has come,
Without the beloved of my heart,
And therefore the blooming green herb
Appears from a distance like the poisonous tongue of a
    serpent.

In the remembrance of the cypress-statured beloved one,
My heart flits about like a dove,
As round about a bright lamp a moth hovers affectionately.
In the garden of this world,
People fill their skirts with roses,
But I, through the road of mine eyes,
Fill my lap with precious blood.

The gardener is sweeping all things,
Buds are opening and blooming,
But of a woman like me, deprived of a husband,
A life of happiness is burnt up.

(20.)

O bright moon of the eyes of this world,
Why hast thou gone away offended with me!
O bright candlestick of a black night,
Why hast thou got tired of me?
In my sorrow from thy separation
Arrow upon arrow issues from my heart.
The quivering breath of my heart
Makes a noise like that of chains.

Alas, alas, O alas! that the "Furhad" of my heart
    has departed,
And I, "Shirin" of a delicate body,
Am crushed by the mountain of separation.

Without thee, O heart-soothing man
The garden of this body is thorny,
The lips of the cup of roses pierce me as swords.

By the water of mine eyes verdure has increased every
    where,
The eggs of the nightingales in their nests
Have changed their colour to yellow.
I have not plucked any fruits or flowers,
Be not angry with me, O gardener,
Know that I have filled these my skirts
With the thorns of my heart only.

Only the birds that have lost their " munsookh"
Give ear to my weeping,
Know thou that their state resembles mine in this garden.

(21.)

I am agonized only through thy separation, O my beloved,
O lover, O heart-comforter, O my beloved,
Having seen thy face I gave my heart ;
This now appears as my crime ;
But after robbing my heart, to be non-existent is thy great
    tyranny.

To wander in thy search day and night
Has become the decree of my fate,
But, O lover, for thee to remain careless
Will never be considered becoming.
I have read a book of thy excellence with the master
    of love,
But in the tale of faithfulness written there
Was great deception.

The ponderous stone of thy tyranny
Hath fallen upon the bottle of this heart,
It has broken it into atoms,
Yet is there faithfulness in it.

Having set thy love upon another world,
Thou hast made my state miserable ;
This world has taken my heart
And made it kubab on the fire of love.

I was filling the eyes of my heart
With the dust of thy love like *surma*,
How did I know that like a wall
It would grow up at once so high ?
Suddenly a great separation took place,
And thy face became invisible.
Pinches of dust heaped up together
And covered up " munsookh," and the health of my body.

(22.)

May no one suffer, in solitude, misery like mine,
My life in solitude endures excessive grief.
Where shall I go ? what shall I do ?
To whom shall I tell my state?
O God, who will attend to my cry in this solitude ?

On account of wakeful nights,
My health is becoming spoiled,
I fill these eyes with blood in solitude.
In the day I wish to complain,
But a sleep of insensibility comes over me.
Women deprived of their husbands
Lose their " munsookh," and suffer afflictions in solitude.

(23.)

O Maker of the rose !
Why hast thou brought calamity on the rose?
Having made it beautiful with the tints of love,
Why hast thou plucked it from the garden ?

Standing in this garden I grieve so excessively,
That the hearts of nightingales and insects weep and
lament.

The roses having torn them, my garments are in a ruined
state,
The garden is overflowing with blood,
Where is the man to remedy it ?
In the expectation of that heart-comforter,
Wherever I open my straitened eyes,
My sight turns backward and stings me like a scorpion.

This time of tasting the sweets,
Is passing in grief and weeping.
Alas ! if the spring passes thus,
Then how will the bad season speed ?
I walk about every morning
In the remembrance of that rose-like face,
Having made my eyes wet like dew,
I wash away all bodily happiness and " munsookh."

(24.)

I will not draw back the hands of my heart,
As long as I have not my desire ;
Either my wish must be gratified,
Or I shall be destroyed from this life.
   (I will not draw back, &c)

As the moth goes round the lantern, about the shining
light,
So wander I, day and night,
In the intoxication of the fire of my love.
   (I will not draw back, &c.)

The road of thy sanctuary is wholly filled with hearts,
Then how shall I, of delicate body,
Talk with thee amid such a concourse ?
   (I will not draw back, &c.)

As a poor man finding a pearl
Hides it from the sight of others,
So take I the ashes of thy sanctuary,
And hide them near these eyes.

    (I will not draw back, &c.)

What wonder if a heart
That has sat in thy sanctuary does not return?
The bird that has sat in the garden
Does not remember its cage.

    (I will not draw back, &c.)

Truly gracious Lord as thou art,
Bestow "munsookh" on helpless me;
Though the colour of roses is fiery,
Yet the thorns are not burnt up.

    (I will not draw back, &c.)

(25.)

Over thy misfortune, O heart,
Thou weepest incessantly in vain,
But as is the decree of nature
So only does any thing happen.
Without weeping, how could I open
The hands of my eyelashes upon thy face?
Without washing, how could I put
My defiled hands to the scriptures?

By tears only my heart has its way pointed out to it,
As by the starry lamps
The pilots find their way on the sea.
Notwithstanding this my greatness,
Tear-drops flow down in streams.
Thanks, to remember a friend,
They serve as a rosary of beads.

I stand in the stream of these tears
Immersed up to the waist.
If thou hast become my enemy,
I also have girded my loins for shedding blood.
In the cradle of these eyes sleep does not find rest,
The children of tears flowing, weeping,
Sit always in their lap.

As newly planted trees have need always of water,
So to me, who am newly absorbed in grief,
There is truly need of weeping.
Without thee, O " munsookh"-like man,
Weeping, distress, doubts, and anxieties,
Come in my heart on every pretence,
And keep me both night and day wakeful.

(26.)

What oppression has thy love exercised upon my heart!
It has robbed me of peace and rest,
And fixed in me pain and grief.
God knows that apart from thee
I have no kind of peace,
By day there is no strength to bear my solitude,
And at night there is no sleep from loneliness.

By thy separation past griefs have revived in my heart,
Do not ask me an account of my pain,
For my diary has been altogether spoiled.
Like a wick in a little lamp,
I keep wet the lashes of mine eyes,
And as the lamp burns through the night,
So weep I all night till the dawn.

A string of tears like a chain,
Is twisted around my neck ;
Some day, leaving the border of my raiment,
It will unexpectedly hang me.

21 A

O, ye eyes, do not cast
These children of tears upon the dust!
For I have spent my life in bringing them up;
I have made them drink the blood of my heart.

As a tear is not afraid of the stormy raging of the sea,
So a woman deprived of her husband,
Having lost " munsookh," is not afraid of the world.

(27.)

The moon and stars shine wonderfully,
Pleasure and singing will be delightful;
How many nights have gone, how many days?
When will the heart-possessor come?
I have sat as it were
In milk on this pleasant moonlight night,
Because by the remembrance of thy black locks,
I was stung as by a black serpent.*

The clear light of the full moon
Is indeed exceedingly pleasant,
But without thee, O angel-faced possessor of my heart,
It is a destroyer of life like the " Sapid Dev."
From love, words sit upon my tongue as lamps;
I speak, I burn, I weep,
And my heart is as black as a wick.

O dear friend of bright countenance,
Without the lustre of thy forehead
My palace even by the sun
Does not become enlightened.

---

* It is said that physicians of eastern countries having given
medicine to a man stung by serpents, sometimes make him sit
in a vessel full of milk that the medicine may have a good
effect upon him. It must be understood that this is the custom
alluded to in the above verse.

By the rising of the sun
The whole world is fully enlightened,
But to the hearts of poor sad moths
It is as it were a grievous darkness.

It is said that in the prayer of the morning
A good man may obtain true " munsookh."
But will my night of grief change to morning !
That a suitable prayer might be offered.

(28.)

In a dark night, palace and garden
Without my lover are a desert,
Vessels and roses too are there,
But without thee my soul does not enjoy them.
At night on account of thy absence alone
My heart is burnt, and my mind disconsolate ;
My eyes remain wakeful
But the drowsiness of sleep rests upon my fate.

The evil night of separation
Does not give an omen of meeting ;
It is a dreadful night of despondency,
When no time of hope is afforded.
The limbs of my distressed body have become so feeble,
That by a breeze of air
My hands and feet tremble as waves.

Through weakness the breath of sighs even
Comes out by little and little,
While coming from the breast to the lips
It rests at a hundred places !
My body has become so thin that the sight of the beholder
Might penetrate to my heart !
Wherever my footsteps are placed,
There they are bound as with chains !

That I am alive this day,
Do not consider the effect of a hard heart,
But my weakness has become so great
That my soul is unable to come to my lips !
Without the beloved one,
Strength stays not in the body of a lover.
Little by little he loses his " munsookh,"
And at the end his life and understanding.

(29.)

Oh my lover ! what a trial thy love is ?
What shall I say in exposing thy unfaithfulness ?
When I draw from my heart
The cold breath of a deep sigh,
Tears get congealed in the goblet of my eyes,
And turn to solid ice !

How can the weak horse of this body,
Withstand the infliction of the stripes of sighs ?
By a heap of grass
How can a flash of bright lightning be hindered ?
As always a touch-stone recognizes only gold,
So in these black eyes thy golden face is all things.

As by the drops of the water of (thawing) ice,
The heart of the sun is not wetted,
So a sea has no effect
Upon the burning heart of a lover.
As upon the bed of an extinguished lamp
There remains a black-coloured smoke,
So nothing remains with a lover after death but sighs.

As to the shop of a bottle maker,
Broken bottles go, and lie there,
So a broken heart, for its cure
Goes to the sanctuary of the beloved.

As from cotton wet with water
A thread cannot be drawn out,
So eyes having become wet with weeping,
The sight is quite shut up.

In the remembrance of the sun of thy face
Stars fall from mine eyes,
By this the world is ruined,
And mine eyes are hurt by thee.
Enter thou by the way of my heart
And sit upon mine eyes,
By the way of the furnace of fire (heart)
Walk around the sea.

Upon the spectacle of thy face
Mine eye is so earnestly fixed
That in the embrace of mine eyelashes
Thoughts of sleep do not rest.
On the banks of the watery fountain
The *subja* of the eyelash grows,
Yet by the inward fire doth it burn and wither.

Varied and beautiful " munsookh"-like words,
The pain of this separation speaks,
In a friendless life nobody will find happiness.

(30.)

To whom shall I show the burning blisters within me?
How long shall I silently suffer
The oppression of thee, my beloved?
On account of thy absence,
This body has become a furnace of fire.
Nobody searches with carefulness
Where the arrows of love are stuck.

So innumerable are the dirhems* of scars,
Which have fallen upon my heart,
That I could easily be a supplier of the world
In the time of scarcity.
As in a ruined house,
No one can long remain at rest,
So little by little will my grief also depart.

O ye nightingales of the garden,
Scatter roses upon me gently,
For in the embrace of this body,
Is the delicate precious bottle of the heart.
At length by the fire of sighs,
Hundreds of clefts have been formed in my heart,
By the waves of the water of mine eyes
The wall of the garden of my body has been undermined.

When the heart rots from disease
It must be kept far from the breast.
However dear a person may die,
Dust has to be cast upon him.
From evening to morning mine eyes count the stars,
The work that belongs to the fingers of my hand,
That mine eyelashes perform.

These eyelashes becoming dry from lack of moisture,
Have separated from mine eyes.
What shall I do with the string
If the pearls themselves have been burnt?
Do not think that the hairy lashes
Upon these eyes are soft,
They are thorns in the feet of mine eyes,
In the road of thy separation!

---

* "Dirhems," (spelt in the usual way of English books,) is
a silver coin worth about three annas.

All religious men tell us
There will be questions and answers at the judgment day,
But these words of "munsookh"
Bring the true judgment day to my mind.

(31.)

I had cherished my heart with various expectations,
But suddenly have I fallen into a pit,
Through lack of carefulness.
How can this heart protect itself
From the wounds of the swords of thy love?
There is no shield upon it, save that of scars.

Lovers bind the fragments of their hearts
With a string of sighs,
And they use it as a rosary
In their prayers day and night.
The scars of my breast,
Having rotted through my tears,
Have turned to running ulcers;
Behold my wretched fate,
My body's rose-garden is burnt by the frost.

Let nobody strike the bottle of my heart
With the stone of reproach;
For, like a drop of quicksilver,
Quivers this restless body.
As from a cracked bottle
An agreeable sound does not come,
So the condition of broken-hearted lovers
Never can be pleasant.

The scars of grief upon the surface of my heart burn,
As fragments of incense in the face of fire.
The running wounds of hearts

Cannot be bound up by physicans,
Even as by the hands of no one
Can the lips of seas be sewn.

Except the afflicted ones
None know the pains of the afflicted,
To roses in which there is no scent
The nightingale pays no honour.
The limbs of this withering body
Do not bloom under the influence of spring,
Like the scars on the heart of the tulip
My black fate remains unchanged.

Without thee the garden has lost
All colour, charm, and fragrance ;
The nightingale murmurs
Taking the blood-red roses in his sight.
Remembering thee, O rose-faced,
I went out to walk in the garden,
But " munsookh" having gone, I wetted mine eyes
As with dew, and then I wept in torrents.

(32.)

Through love for thee a mountain of grief
Has suddenly fallen upon my head,
I have lost the peace and joy of this life,
And suffered great afflictions.
As without their parents little children do not go out,
So without the fragments of the heart,
Streams of tears do not flow.

The waters of these eyes both day and night,
Wash the scars of this my heart,
Remembering thee, without weeping,

Is like prayer without ablution.
To see thy face the feet of these mine eyes,
Run so much by day and night that they are sprained.

From the mountain as it were of my heart,
The fountain of my tears issues,
But by the flood of this very fountain,
I will sweep away that mountain.
These tears, on account of thy absence,
Have gradually become a sea ;
Sit thou in the boat of this eye,
And come here quickly for an excursion.

The water of weeping
Makes clear my blood-filled eyes,
As the dew of night, like oil,
Keeps bright the lamp of a tulip.
These children of tears pluck fragrant roses
From the garden of the heart,
And like a gardener's basket mine eye
Has become a receptacle for flowers.

From my eyes how can
The scalding, flowing water of tears be stopped ?
There is no power in any man to prevent the rain.
As the head of a slanderer is hung upon the gallows,
So for the crime of divulging secrets,
Tears hang upon the eyelashes.

This my weak body has fallen,
Far away from the rose of thy face.
Into the neck of my soul, as it were,
Poisonous thorns are piercing.
The full moon has gone, but alas,
The night of grief has not gone,
It is fixed as it were with a nail
Among the stars of darkness.

25 A

I dreamed at night that
Thy " munsookh''-like countenance would quickly
    meet me,
At which the night of my grief became bright as the day.

(33.)

I wish for thy company—thou desirest solitude,
How then can I show thee the attachment of my heart?
O beloved, pure love of any kind
Doth not appear in thee,
For in the goblet of my life
Thou hast thrown the agonizing poison of separation.

Through this bitterness,
The oppressive plunderer, death, is as it were, so scared,
That he makes no assault to rob my precious life.
Without thee the blood of these eyes is my wine,
The frenzy of my heart burns like a lamp at a banquet.

Burning with fire day and night,
I make all the blood of my body ashes,—
But by some strange means
No sign whatever of smoke is seen there.
The whole sense of my heart is stolen,
All knowledge and patience are stolen.
What value must be set on my thief?
For he has taken both
The treasure and the abode of my soul!

In the atmosphere of the garden of love
I became a flying cloud with passion.
I did not pluck the flower of hope,
And like dew fell upon the ground.

The thought of thee only is in my heart,
I am the heart myself.
Of senselessness, misery, and unprofitableness,
This my heart has become a home.

With the remembrance of thy words,
My ears having been filled,
Mine eyes have become empty ;
Come, for it is now a matter of life,
And my soul has come even to my lips.
On the mirror of the cup of this breast,
The breath of hope still lingers.
If thou wouldst take the trouble to meet me,
My state would become enlightened.

My soul flies toward thee,
And my distracted heart wanders here ;
The dry grass of my body, is as it were,
Drawn in opposite ways, by two pieces of amber.
Thou didst purpose taking a journey,
And made my heart sorrowful,
Thou didst gird up the loins of thy courage,
And rooted out mine altogether.

O light of mine eyes, thou hast gone,
And these eyes are here without light.
Thou hast left me in a forest of darkness,
And hast gone away from the city.
At the time of thy journey,
Weeping was a lock on my lips,
Although I desired to speak,
I could not utter even a word.

Thou wentest on thy journey with pleasure,
Leaving me here wounded ;
Having severed our affection,
Without reason thou took'st grief's calm away with thee.

Forsaking thy own bright country,
Thou wentest suddenly to a foreign shore.
Therefore do mine eyes turn round and round,
Revolving like the stars.

O possessor of my heart, strange is the quality
Of the fire of thy separation,
The further and further it goes,
The more and more it burns.
Through incessant crying
Innumerable blisters have come upon this tongue,
In the sea of my sorrowful eyes,
" Munsookh" and rest have been drowned.

(34.)

This truly is the subject
Of my prayer day and night,
That by striving with my body and mind,
I may obtain the beloved of my heart.
Alms from the house of a well wishing friend,
Are better than a kingdom.
By the remembrance of thy actual love,
The world appears altogether unfaithful.

Ever since I reposed
The head of my heart on this place,
This light of the lofty sun has been my pillow.
None has seen thy face,
While lakhs of souls are thy lovers.
Though thou art hidden like a bud,
Yet the nightingales lose their senses.

I will become soft and black coloured ashes upon thy altar,
For there is no venturing to approach thee,
Save in the shape of ashes.

The body is ashes, the soul ashes,
Water and fire are also ashes,
Without thee all things are ashes,
Without thee even " munsookh " is ashes.

(35.)

ADDRESS TO THE DEITY.—AN ODE.

Upon my wretchedness look with pity,
Since Thou only art the heart-soother of the world ;
Grant the desires of this poor one, me,
For Thou only art the true provider.

(Upon my wretchedness look, &c.)

If the reflection of the light of thy love
Were to fall upon me,
I should be fully exalted to the heaven like the sun.

(Upon my wretchedness look, &c.)

If the Homa bird of Thy favour
Were to fly upon my head,
Then the moon, stars, and the whole world
Would receive light from me.

(Upon my wretchedness look, &c.)

Before whom shall I speak my words ?
Since Thou only art the restorer,
From whom may I expect redress of my griefs ?
Since Thou art both the worlds' great king.

(Upon my wretchedness look, &c.)

I humbly cling as dust
To the skirts of thy garment,
Lift me up with the breeze of Thy love,
And make me reach Thy sanctuary,

(Upon my wretchedness look, &c.)

There is no need of making
A representation of grievances in Thy presence,
Nobody's secrets and designs,
And nobody's shame are hidden from Thee.

(Upon my wretchedness look, &c.)

Though I am in poor circumstances,
What doth it matter?
If Thou art the remedy of all griefs,
Of what use is it to seek another?

(Upon my wretchedness look, &c.)

On every occasion I have
Need of Thy favours only,
Whether my conduct or works
Be meritorious, or bad or good.

(Upon my wretchedness look, &c.)

By the alchemy of Thy love,
Turn the dust of my actions into gold,
For times and seasons, and grace and wrath,
Are in the hands of Thy infinite power.

(Upon my wretchedness look, &c.)

Thou art worthy of all command,
I am thy order-bearer,
Hundreds of foes would be discomfited,
If the crown of Thy friendship were upon my head.

(Upon my wretchedness look, &c.)

I am keeping in this heart,
All things reminding me of Thee,
And this eye, I have filled,
With the pure pearls of Thy favour.

(Upon my wretchedness look, &c.)

I am far from Thee in body,
But my spirit is near Thee,
Whether I am worthy or not worthy,
Yet my services are bestowed upon Thee only.

      (Upon my wretchedness look, &c.)

Wherever I look in this world,
A fondness for Thy worship arises.
Since both the worlds are Thy abode,
How can I place confidence in another ?

      (Upon my wretchedness look, &c.)

Wherever I walk in body or in mind,
There all authority is Thine,
Whether I am near or whether I am far,
I am still the ashes of Thy sanctuary.

      (Upon my wretchedness look, &c.)

Though Thou art hidden from my eyes,
Thou existest in my soul.
Sitting, lying down, my soul cries
Day and night, O Thou, O Thou !

      (Upon my wretchedness look, &c.)

In the circle of Thy dominion,
I am like a point of the compass,
Thou canst show love, show wrath,
Or make my hand exalted.

      (Upon my wretchedness look, &c.)

In faithfulness and friendship,
I am pure gold of the finest quality ;
Test me as Thou pleasest with the touchstone,
Thou wilt find no defect in me.

      (Upon my wretchedness look, &c.)

Make me happy, lessen my grief,
And remove my anxiety of mind,
Grant me love in my soul,
Fondness in my heart,
And the remembrance of " munsookh" in my lips.

(36.)

PETITION TO THE ALMIGHTY.—AN ODE.

I have fixed my mind upon Thee only,
O Lord, pure and bountiful Creator,
Thou art the Lord of Great Power,
The whole earth and heaven depend upon Thee.

(I have fixed my mind, &c.)

Upon the moon, sun, stars, water,
Wind, mountains, beasts and birds,
Whales, fishes, insects, and men,
Thy boundless favours rest.

(I have fixed my mind, &c.)

All powerful and incomparable art Thou,
Ever revealed yet ever hidden.
Do good unto me,
O world's life, O world's Lord, holy provider.

(I have fixed my mind, &c.)

Highest of all, greatest supporter !
O merciful, O bounteous, show me mercy,
Remove every fear and misery,
And lay upon me the weight of happiness.

(I have fixed my mind, &c.)

Truly bending my head with shame,
I have surrendered myself,
Hold this base hand with love and encouragement,
And bear me safely through this world.

(I have fixed my mind, &c.)

Whatever petition I ask of Thee,
That do Thou fully grant,
With justice and mercy put away my distresses,
And keep my heart religious.

(I have fixed my mind, &c.)

Preserve my reputation in the world,
And lengthen my life.
My fame, well being, and righteous action,
All do Thou, O Lord, sustain.

(I have fixed my mind, &c.)

Thou only art the coverer of sins,
Thou only the forgiver,
Thou the beginning, Thou the end,
Thou art above, Thou art beneath,
Thou art all righteousness and love !

(I have fixed my mind, &c.)

Imperfect, imperfect, the whole world is imperfect,
Except Thee, all is imperfect !
Ended—ended—"Munsookh's" work is ended,
But Thy name and work endure for ever !!!

(I have fixed my mind, &c.)

FINIS.

www.ingramcontent.com/pod-product-compliance
Lightning Source LLC
Chambersburg PA
CBHW032007060726
47497CB00017B/2374